In Darkling Wood

In Darkling Wood

Emma Carroll

Delacorte Press

Text copyright © 2015 by Emma Carroll
Jacket art copyright © 2017 by Kate Forrester

All rights reserved. Published in the United States by Delacorte Press, an imprint of Random House Children's Books, a division of Penguin Random House LLC, New York.

Originally published in trade paperback by Faber & Faber Limited, an imprint of Bloomsbury House, London, in 2015.

Delacorte Press is a registered trademark and the colophon is a trademark of Penguin Random House LLC.

randomhousekids.com

Educators and librarians, for a variety of teaching tools, visit us at RHTeachersLibrarians.com

Library of Congress Cataloging-in-Publication Data
Carroll, Emma.
In darkling wood / Emma Carroll. —First American edition.
pages cm
"Originally published by Faber & Faber, An imprint of Bloomsbury House, London, in 2015"
Summary: When Alice goes to stay with her grandmother she discovers the magic of Darkling Wood, where she meets a strange friend and discovers letters written between a brother and sister during WWI.
ISBN 978-0-399-55601-2 (hc) — ISBN 978-0-399-55603-6 (ebook)
[1. Magic—Fiction. 2. Fairies—Fiction. 3. Brothers and sisters—Fiction. 4. Letters—Fiction. 5. World War, 1914–1918—Fiction. 6. Fantasy.] I. Title.
PZ7.1C426 In2016
[Fic]—dc23
2015049623

The text of this book is set in 12-point Amasis.
Interior design by Heather Kelly

Printed in the United States of America
10 9 8 7 6 5 4 3
First American Edition

To Owen,
who gave this story idea wings

1

Monday, 11 November

At 3:23 a.m., the hospital calls to say a heart's been found. Put like that, it almost sounds funny, as if someone's just discovered it in a rubbish bin or on a doorstep, like happens in the news sometimes with tiny babies.

Except that's not how it is.

What they really mean is someone's died. A stranger, carrying a donor card, has stopped living. It's hard not to think of that person's family and what the hospital had to tell them tonight. Yet without that donor heart my little brother will stop living too.

So for once, I think we're the lucky ones.

The first I know of it is a beeping noise near my head. It's my brother Theo's favorite and most annoying joke. Last time he set my alarm clock for three a.m. I got him back by putting cheese in his pillowcase. But nowadays it's mostly me who's washing the bed linen and buying the cheese, so I'm a bit more sensible.

The beeping goes on. It's not my clock. And as my brain catches up, I remember I can't blame Theo either. These past few weeks he's slept in the dining room because he can't climb the stairs anymore. Once we'd moved his bed in and put up his *Doctor Who* posters, it looked like a normal kid's bedroom, if you ignored the oxygen tank and the plastic box full of pills.

The beeping is coming from the room next door. It sounds like Mum's pager, the one given to her for emergencies. My stomach goes into knots.

There's a thud. An "Ouch!" The beeping stops.

I hear Mum's door open. That creaky third step tells me she's going downstairs. The kitchen light clicks on and she starts talking fast. I lie very still to listen.

"We'll be there, Doctor," says Mum.

Two years ago, Theo blew out his birthday cake candles in one big puff, then collapsed right in front of us on the carpet. We thought he was mucking about at first, but then his lips went blue like they do when you've been swimming in the sea too long.

When the ambulance came Mum tried to be cheerful; she even offered the paramedics some of Theo's cake. Then came the hospital tests—X-rays, scans, needles that left bruises on the back of Theo's hands; it got harder to stay cheerful after that. A virus had attacked my brother's heart, so the doctors said, which apparently can happen to anyone. Except Theo isn't "anyone": this stupid, random thing has happened to us.

There's a different sort of beeping now as Mum sends a text. Then she's waking Theo. I can't hear her actual words, but her voice is high-pitched like she's telling him we're going somewhere exciting. Next she's back upstairs, opening my door.

"Alice?" Mum hisses. "You awake?"

I am. Wide-awake. Like she's chucked water in my face.

"What's happening?" I say.

"A heart's become available."

My stomach knots get tighter. I wriggle up the bed and turn on the bedside lamp.

"And is it . . . ?"

Mum leans against the doorframe. Her hair is all on end. She's smiling and crying at the same time.

"Yes," she says. "It's a perfect match."

Twenty minutes later, we're in the car. The hospital is in London, which is 110 miles south down the motorway. We'll need to get a move on because a donor heart doesn't last long. They pack it in ice and inject it with potassium to stop it beating. After that, it's only good for four to six hours.

Theo sits in the back, oxygen line in his nose. He's managed to sneak his dinosaur toys in with him; there are T. rexes and diplodocuses and triceratopses all over the seat.

"You'll have to give those to Mum when we get there, buddy," I say as I fasten my seat belt.

"Will I, Mum?" Theo sounds worried.

Mum looks in the rearview mirror. "Don't worry, love. I've heard nurses are *big* dinosaur fans."

Then she glares at me.

"What?" I say. "It said 'no toys' in that booklet from the hospital because of germs."

"I *know* that," says Mum, but I'm guessing she'd rather not think about it. There are so many things that could go wrong, and the booklet lists quite a few.

"Can't we think of something nice, like . . . I don't know . . . chocolate cake or Christmas or . . ."

". . . unicorns and fairies . . ." I slouch down in my seat.

"All right, I get it."

We take the main road through town, passing shops, then pubs, then takeaways. Mum's driving faster than normal.

"Aren't you dropping me at Lexie's?" I say, as we don't take the turning to my best friend's house. Ever since we knew Theo needed a transplant, this has been the plan. The hospital has space for Mum to stay, but not me.

"Sorry, love." She pats my knee. "I texted her mum, but she can't have you tonight. She thinks the baby's on its way. Great timing, huh?"

I stare out the window. Bite down on my lip. *No tears. Not now.*

"You're disappointed, aren't you?" Mum says.

I shrug. Staying at Lexie's is a treat these days. It happens so rarely, what with Mum working and Theo being ill. But now the baby's coming and Lexie'll be so excited that I can't feel bad about it. And Kate, her poor mum, looks ready to burst.

"So am I coming to the hospital?" I ask.

"Just till we sort something out."

I don't much like the sound of this. I mean, it's not like I can stay with Dad or anything. Not unless she fancies sending me all the way to Devon.

"I'd be fine at home on my own, you know. I *can* look after myself," I tell her.

"I don't doubt it for a minute, sweetie," Mum says. "But you're under sixteen, so the law advises that you shouldn't be left alone overnight."

A sinking feeling hits my stomach. This isn't the sort of thing my mother normally knows. Or says.

2

The motorway is almost empty. It starts to rain. Theo's gone quiet in the back, so I swivel around to check he's all right. He's fast asleep, a T. rex in each hand. I look closer just to check he's still breathing. I don't tell anyone I do this, but lately I've been checking an awful lot.

As we get nearer London, there's more traffic. The roads sound hissy because of the rain. Just after six a.m., we pull up outside a huge old building with lights on at most of its windows. The hospital looks different at this time of day, like a hotel or a smart block of flats.

Mum lifts Theo from the car. He's still asleep, so thankfully there's no tussle over dinosaurs; I ease the T. rexes out of his hands. The rest stay in the car along with the stuff I'd brought for Lexie's. We enter the hospital through sliding doors, Mum with one arm hooked around Theo, the other pulling the little trolley thing that holds his oxygen. The doors close behind us. It's bright and hot inside. There's the hum of floor polishers and a smell of antiseptic and cooking mixed together. We go up to where a man sits almost hidden behind a desk.

"Hello, we're an emergency admission," Mum says. "The name's Theo Campbell. Cheetah Ward."

The man takes ages checking his screen. Mum shifts Theo onto her hip. I can tell she's dead nervous. She catches my eye and winks, which is her way of asking if I'm okay. I try to smile back but my stomach's churning. Suddenly Mum stares over the top of Theo's head.

"Oh my word. This must be her!"

I turn around to see a woman I don't recognize in a long dark coat. She's standing in the entrance. Behind her, the sliding doors keep opening and shutting.

Mum goes over. "Nell!" she cries.

I follow. Up close, the woman looks old—not seriously old, but older than Mum. She's very thin and tall, with gray hair in a plait over one shoulder. Pinned to her jacket is one of those Remembrance Day poppies. Then I notice her hands. They're enormous, like a scarecrow's. There's dirt under her nails. She still hasn't moved. The doors open-close open-close. Letting go of Theo's trolley, Mum beckons her forward. At last the doors slide shut. "Thank you *so* much for coming at such short notice," Mum says. "I didn't know who else to call."

"I suppose you tried David?" the woman says.

My ears prick up because David is Dad's name. Nearly three years ago, he took a job designing houses made of wood, which meant moving to Devon. But Mum said she didn't want to live somewhere that had more cows than people. If Dad wanted us to go with him, she said, then they should get married since they'd put it off for long enough. But instead of a proposal, there was shouting. In the end, Dad went to Devon on his own.

"I've left a message," Mum says. "But I expect he's still asleep."

The woman snorts. "There'll be some excuse. There always is."

I don't like her saying this, not when we haven't seen much of Dad lately. He's been busy with work, so he says, and with his new baby daughter. Now I'm wondering if these are excuses too.

"Nell, you remember Alice, my eldest?" Mum says, a bit too brightly. I can tell she's struggling to stay calm.

But the woman keeps staring at Mum. "It's been a long time, Carrie—ten years, maybe?" The woman keeps talking. She has a rich-sounding voice. No one in our family sounds like that—well, only Dad. It's then I work out who she is. As my mouth drops open, Mum introduces us.

"Alice, this is your grandmother from your father's side. You've not seen her since you were little. But she's going to look after you for a bit and we're grateful, aren't we?"

Grateful? The woman's a total stranger! I don't remember her at all. Leaning in to Mum, I hiss in her ear, "I'd be fine on my own. You know I would."

"Sorry, sweetie," Mum whispers back. "Nell's all right, really. Just do your best. You won't be with her for long."

"Can't I come with you? I won't get in the way."

Mum sighs. "Alice, we've been through this. There's only accommodation here for me. It's a busy ward. There's no space for patients' sisters."

I bite my lip to stop it wobbling. Behind us, a phone rings. Deep inside her handbag, Mum's emergency pager beeps. The man at the desk calls over.

"Hello? They need you now. They're ready for him in theater."

Instantly I feel bad for being pathetic. Theo groans in Mum's arms and starts to wake up. He rubs his eyes, then does his usual wet cough. Out of habit, I check his line. It's fine. It's always fine; the problem isn't with the oxygen.

Mum puts her free arm around me. She smells of home. "I'll phone you as soon as it's over."

"When can I visit?"

"In a day or so, hopefully."

It's all happening too quickly. I'm not ready to leave. Theo looks pale and sleepy, like a little animal nestled up against Mum.

"Be brave, bro," I say, trying hard not to cry. "I'll see you very soon."

"Promise, Alice?" he says.

"Promise."

"Really, *really* promise?"

"With bells on."

He sighs and shuts his eyes.

My stuff! I think suddenly. It's still in the car. The man at reception is trying to hurry Mum. She looks flustered and almost drops Theo as she searches one-handedly for her keys. As usual, they're right at the bottom of her bag. Her fingers shake as she hands them over.

"I'll leave them at the front desk," I say. Backing away, Mum blows me a kiss.

"Call you," she says.

By the time I've got my bags, then dropped Mum's keys at reception, there's no sign of Nell in the hospital. Eventually I see her waiting for me on the opposite side of the street. She starts walking as soon as I join her.

"Are we going straight home?" I say.

"Yes."

I nod, relieved. At least I'll be in my own house, in my own bed. And I'll see Lexie later at school, which'll help. We cross another street and go into a car park. She starts unlocking a car that looks even older than ours.

In the backseat something moves. It makes me jump.

"You're not scared of dogs, are you?" Nell says.

I'm not. But this one's massive. As Nell opens my door and I get in, I'm hit by the doggy smell.

"He really is a dear thing," Nell says, reaching around to smooth the dog's head.

"But our house isn't that big," I say. "And he's ... well ... huge."

Nell starts the car. "We're not going to your house, Alice. You're coming home with me, to my house. Didn't your mother explain?"

"No," I say, gritting my teeth. "She didn't."

3

By the time the journey is over, I know not to call her Grandma or Nanny or Nan: her name is Nell. She doesn't say anything about Dad, only that she hates hospitals. When I ask why, she pulls a face.

"Yuck," she says. "Just yuck."

The stinky dog is called Borage. He's gray and shaggy and has doggy eyebrows, and he leans like a human when we take corners. So this is who I'm spending the next I-don't-know-how-long with. Honestly, I'd have been far better off at home on my own.

We've driven two hours out of London to reach Nell's house. It's daylight now. The last few miles are on country lanes that actually have grass growing down the middle. I lose the signal on my phone. Things really don't look promising. Then the road splits into two. We take the right-hand part, which quickly turns into a track and goes very steeply downhill. It carries on like this for a bone-shaking half a mile, then stops at a five-bar gate. The house is just beyond, surrounded by trees: both look really old. The building is made of gray stone, with funny arched windows and a front door so wide and dark it makes me think of castles. It's called Darkling Cottage; the name's nailed to the gate in brass letters. "Darkling": it's a funny word. Old-sounding.

"Why's it called that?" I ask.

"It gets its name from those woods." Nell points to the trees that surround the house on three sides. "Suits it, don't you think?"

I don't know. It sounds spooky to me.

"Did Dad bring us to visit when we were little?" I ask. "Because I don't remember it if he did."

"No. He didn't," she says.

As I open my mouth to ask "Why?" Nell gets in there first.

"You ask a lot of questions," she says. I'd asked precisely two and a half.

"Open the gate, will you?" says Nell. "And let the dog out of the car."

I do as she asks. Borage lollops off on great gangly legs, looking more like a baby horse than a dog.

Once Nell's parked up, I get my bags and follow her around to the back of the house. It's a fine, bright morning but the sun hasn't reached here yet. Everything is still white with frost. I suppose the trees make it so shadowy; they come right up to the garden fence on all three sides. The garden itself looks well cared for, not like ours at home, which at the moment is ankle deep in dead leaves.

"Do you like gardening?" I say, then realize I've just asked another question.

Nell gets that same look she had when we talked about hospitals.

"If I had a garden worth tending, yes," she says. "See there, where the ground's lifted?"

She points to our side of the fence. All along it, the grass looks rough and lumpy, especially closest to the house.

"Tree roots." She tosses her head as she says it, like she really hasn't got time for all this. "If the blasted things grow any nearer to the house it'll be dangerous."

"How?"

"An old house like mine doesn't have deep foundations, so if the tree roots grow too close and make the soil dry it causes the house to become unstable, you see. It's called subsidence. The trees themselves aren't stable, either. All we'd need is a decent storm, and any one of them could come crashing down on the house."

"Oh," I say nervously. "Right."

"That's the worst-case scenario, of course, but they're such a blasted nuisance, taking goodness from the soil and making everywhere so dark. That's why I've decided to cut down the wood."

"You're cutting down the *whole thing*?" It seems a bit dramatic.

"Don't look so horrified," Nell says. "It's only three acres of land—*my* land, I hasten to add."

We stand silent, looking at the trees. They're old and twisty and so tall I have to tip my head back to see them properly. Right at the top are crows' nests; we've startled them. They fly above us, making a miserable croaking noise that sends a shiver through me.

"You're cold. Go on inside," says Nell, handing me the door key. "I'll be in shortly for breakfast."

Before I get a chance to ask which bedroom is mine, she's striding off across the lawn.

Inside, the house feels really old. Unsure where to put

myself, I dump my bags in the hallway. Nell's right, it *is* dark in here—so dark I have to put the lights on.

More importantly, there's no Internet. No telly. And still no mobile signal, so I can't call Lexie to see if she's become a sister yet.

There are three massive downstairs rooms, all freezing cold and smelling of damp, and a kitchen that's the size of a classroom. I settle in here; it's got one of those old cookers you put coal into, which makes it the warmest room by a mile.

All morning, I keep the kitchen door propped open so I can hear the phone in the hall when Mum rings. Borage lies across my feet like a giant, hairy hot-water bottle. Time goes slower than slow. Yet my brain's zipping about all over the place, and when I try to read a book or do homework I can't concentrate on anything. In the end, I make Theo a get-well card on some paper I find in my schoolbag. At least now I've got something to take him when I visit. Not that I can draw, but he'll like it because I've done it, though my T. rexes look more like killer pigs.

Finally Mum calls at just after two.

"It's all over," she says. "The operation went brilliantly. He's such a brave chap."

We both have a cry down the phone. It's the relief, I suppose. Then Mum switches back into cheerful mode.

"Are you okay?" she says, sniffing back her tears.

"I'm fine. Did you get hold of Dad?"

There's a pause. "I've left him another message. He was probably in his workshop and didn't hear the phone."

I think of what Nell said about excuses. Now Mum's making them *for* Dad, which, frankly, is weird.

"How are things with Nell?" Mum asks.

"The house is really old. There's no central heating or Internet or anything."

"Oh heck, *really*?"

I don't say much more because I don't want her worrying, so it ends up with Mum babbling on. Maybe I'm a bit on edge but it's like she's trying too hard to sound normal.

The day drags on. There's nothing to do here. Then there's dinner. Nell takes something from the freezer and microwaves it on "high." We end up with what looks like beef but it's so rubbery I have to swallow it down with water. By the time Nell's finished I'm not even halfway through mine.

"You're a picky eater, I see," she says. "Your father was fussy with food too. . . ."

She stops like she's caught herself out. Not that I want her to talk about Dad. Just the mention of him makes me want to kick something. How could he not answer his stupid phone, today of all days?

Nell sees I'm upset. She doesn't say any more about the dinner I've barely touched and instead makes me a coffee with extra sugar.

"I'll be in the library doing paperwork," she says, and disappears.

For a while I sit, head in hands, feeling all sorts of miserable. Then there's a shuffling under the table and Borage's whiskery gray snout rests on my knee. Outside, the wind makes a strange humming noise in the trees. I can't imagine growing up here like Dad did, in a house miles from anywhere with no TV and no heating.

Right now, I can't even imagine Dad. When he first went to Devon, I remember Mum crying and our recycling box being full of wine bottles. We saw him once a month at weekends, which felt weird. When Theo first got sick, I think we hoped Dad would come home. But he didn't. He'd been gone two years by then, and he had a girlfriend called Lara.

This summer they had a baby together, a little girl called Poppy. We haven't met her yet, Theo and me, because since she's been born our dad has been ever so, ever so busy.

Or, as Nell puts it, he started making excuses.

4

It's nighttime now. I'm in bed wearing PJs, socks, two sweaters, and the bobble hat that I knitted myself and am quite proud of. I don't think I've ever been this cold in my life. Nell's put me in the attic room at the very top of the house. It's done up in this ancient-looking wallpaper that makes your eyes go funny because it's line after line of yellow roses. There are no heaters in here. There's not even a duvet. Instead, I've got blankets and stripy sheets and a narrow iron bed that looks like it's out of *Oliver Twist*. It's not exactly cozy.

Hospitals, on the other hand, are always warm. I wonder if Theo's awake or asleep right now. Either way, Mum'll be with him. Perhaps the hospital where Lexie's mum is giving birth lets sisters on the ward, or maybe it's only Kate's partner who's allowed. My mum gets to sleep on a sofa bed in Theo's room: the booklet from Cheetah Ward said so. And I'm glad he's not alone, but it's odd being here without them, like I've got this empty space all around me where usually there's Theo and Mum.

In the end, I go downstairs in search of a hot-water bottle.

But going through the cupboards all I find is dried pasta and dog food. There's no sign of anything helpful. I can't believe Nell doesn't die of cold. Or starvation. Or both.

I'm about to give up and go upstairs when Borage starts scratching at the back door. I suppose he wants to go out.

"Off you go, then," I say, opening the door for him. "And don't be long."

But instead of going out he stands up on his hind legs, puts his paws on my shoulders, and tries to lick my face.

"Arrggh! Get off!"

His nose is in my hair and I'm panicking and laughing at the same time. What the heck is he *doing*? It almost knocks me off my feet. Then he drops down and he's off across the lawn, looking like he's got something in his mouth.

I wait on the doorstep. Somewhere in the dark, a fox barks. At least, I think that's what it is. Perhaps it's a scream or a baby crying, I wouldn't know. I can't see a thing either. This darkness is total, not like at home where there's streetlights and the sky's purple so you can't see the stars. Here it's like staring into a hole.

Bit by bit my eyes get used to it. I can just about see as far as the fence, where the wood starts like a great big wall of black. There's no sign of Borage, though, and I get this sinking feeling that he's found a rabbit or whatever it is dogs chase. I wait a bit longer. Hug myself because I'm getting cold again. He doesn't appear. It's then, as I tuck my hair behind my ears, that I realize I'm no longer wearing my bobble hat.

It could've come off inside the house. But then I think of how Borage went off across the lawn all pleased with himself. That pesky dog's got it, that's where it is.

I call to Borage but it gets lost against the noise the wind is making in the trees. It's no good; I'm going to have to go looking for him. Stupid dog, I think as I stumble across the lawn. And stupid me for letting him out here in the first place. Nell won't be happy if I've lost him. I'm beginning to wish I'd never got out of bed.

Finding the fence is easy enough. There should be a gate here somewhere; I saw one this morning. But it takes a bit of walking up and down before I find it. It's latched shut, though a dog Borage's size could easily jump it, so it wouldn't hurt to look on the other side.

I hesitate.

The wood is darker than anything. What's the point in looking when I won't be able to see a thing? I might get lost. Or sprain my ankle.

Or something.

I'm not scared, though. Not as scared as I'll be if I have to tell Nell I've lost her dog.

Taking a deep breath, I open the gate. It leads onto what feels like a path because the ground is smooth and flat, though it's too dark to tell. Pretty quickly I'm fighting my way through brambles. They scratch at my hair and face, and when I put my arms up to protect myself they snag my sweaters too. The path seems to run out, and I'm now walking blind into what feels like one gigantic hedge. It's ridiculous. I stop, turn around, call Borage again. To my right, something rustles in the bushes. Thank goodness.

"Good dog! Come on!" I listen hard.

No dog comes bounding out of the dark. The rustling

stops. I'm about to call again when I hear a crunch, the sound of footsteps on dead leaves. My heart starts to pound.

This is stupid. What am I doing here? Borage must know these woods inside out. He'll find his way home.

Yet I fight the urge to run. I'm not a chicken. It's only a load of old trees. Making myself breathe normally, I walk back toward the gate. I'm nearly there, nearly calm again, when to my left I see something white flicker between the trees. Quick as it appears, it's gone.

There's someone else in this wood.

My sensible self kicks in: *Go to bed. Get Nell.*

I rush at the gate. The latch won't open. My fingers fumble and slip. "Come on, come on," I hiss under my breath.

At last the gate opens and I'm out on the lawn. It feels like safety, until I see that the kitchen light is on and Nell is silhouetted on the doorstep.

"What are you doing, you silly girl!" she cries.

As I get closer, I see she's wearing old-man-style pajamas. Her arms are folded across her chest.

I squeeze past her in the doorway.

"Where's Borage?" she says.

"I thought he wanted the toilet. He was scratching at the door and then he . . ."

"So you let him outside, is that it?"

"I didn't know he would run off. But he took my hat and I went looking for him and . . ."

Nell raises her eyebrows.

". . . and I thought someone was out there," I say, realizing how rubbish it sounds.

"In the woods?"

I nod. My stupid eyes fill up.

She sighs. "It's those frightful trees, that's what spooked you. The sooner they're cleared the better."

Nell shouts Borage's name and he appears almost immediately, going straight to his bed by the stove. There's no sign of my lovely hat. Slamming the back door shut, Nell herds me up the stairs.

"Now go to sleep," she says.

I'm glad to get into bed; I can cry now without anyone seeing. Pulling the blankets tight around me, I decide I hate it here. If I tell Mum tomorrow then perhaps she'll come and get me. This makes me feel a tiny bit better.

Darkling Cottage
Monday, 11 November, 1918

Dear Alfred,

What magnificent news! The war is over! This must mean your regiment is coming home. Though Papa has warned me not to shriek every time the gate clicks because France is quite some distance away.

As you know, I'm not good at waiting. So I've decided to write to you, though you mustn't mock—my penmanship isn't neat like yours, but I do promise to write very often.

Today was all about celebrating, though not before I'd had orders to smarten myself up. You'll remember how muddy the woods are at this time of year, and how the lane down to the house runs with water when it rains hard. Mama's grown so sick of mud on my skirts, she's close to stopping me from going out altogether.

If you ask me, it's skirts that should be stopped, not muddy walks.

Once I'd passed inspection, Mama and I set off to the village. We didn't take the trap because poor Ginger's still slightly lame. So by the time we'd walked through the woods and crossed Glossop's meadow you can imagine how we looked. Ma's skirt hems were soaked and my best boots filthier than the ones I'd left at home.

At eleven o'clock precisely, the church bells rang and our entire village filled the streets. Oh Alfred, you should've seen it! Everyone was waving flags and singing "For he's a jolly good fellow." I supposed they meant the landlord of the White Lamb, who was handing out free cider. But Mama said they were singing for our prime minister, Mr. Lloyd George.

The bells rang for an hour without stopping. Imagine the agony to our ears! It's probably why Mrs. Burgess brought the schoolchildren out to listen. Though you'll hardly believe it but our dear old headmistress was actually SMILING.

She made a point of coming over and simpering at Mama—it was all "yes, Mrs. Waterhouse, no, Mrs. Waterhouse"—though she didn't once address me; I made sure of it by taking a great interest in my coat buttons.

Afterwards, Mama asked where my manners had gone. It was time I acted more like a young lady, she said. Perhaps I could pin my hair up and swap my frocks for blouses and skirts. Well, I must have scowled because she laughed and said being ladylike wasn't so terrible.

But it is terrible, Alfred. I hate it when things have to change. Sometimes I'm even envious of that farm dog for how it roams around our woods without a care, though I'd not want Mr. Glossop for a master.

As for Papa, he is still recovering from his time at the

Front. Mostly, he sits all day and reads—ghost stories are his favorite—which Mama rolls her eyes at because she says they're what servants read. She thinks he needs a hobby, something to "take his mind off things." But I don't know if it helps, this not mentioning the war. After all, he has shrapnel in his leg that will never go away, and he still screams in the night.

Sorry to sound dismal. Mostly I stay jolly by thinking of what we'll do when you come home. We'll climb the beech tree and sit in our favorite spot, where the branch splits and makes that funny O shape. We'll take a picnic too, only this time I promise not to eat all the apple cake without sharing.

Actually, I can't promise that. Even now there is rationing, Mrs. Cotter's baking is still scrumptious. She's already making lists of what to cook when you come home. She and Maisie have been saving up the rations—"stockpiling," Mama called it, when she found more sugar in our larder than we'd had in months. So, Alfred, do be sure to come home hungry. It would be torture to have to eat all that cake alone.

And think of the woods, Alfred! Never mind that it's winter, they're still our special place. It'll be wonderful to have you here again. Not like before, when you came home on leave for just two weeks. This time you'll stay for good.

Your sister

5

Tuesday, 12 November

"Good grief, is that toast *dry*?" Nell says at breakfast the next morning.

I nod and gulp; there's nothing in the cupboards to put on it, and better dry toast than nothing.

She rolls her eyes. Pulling a ten-pound note from her shirt pocket, she hands it to me. "There's a shop in the village. Get what you need."

I think she's trying to be nice. Or maybe she just doesn't want to be held responsible for me starving to death.

The village is called Bexton. It's about two miles away, through the woods and across some fields. Borage comes with me, though after last night I'm surprised Nell trusts me with her dog.

"Just make sure you bring him back in one piece" is all she says.

As I set off, I feel my mood lift. It's better to be doing something. I hate sitting around, waiting for news from Mum. Darkling Wood looks different this morning. The trees are bare because it's winter, and as the sun sparkles through their branches, I can almost see to the fields beyond. It's so quiet here. No cars. No buses. No radios blaring. An airplane passes overhead, but even that's silent.

All along the fence are the trees Nell says will be cut down first because their roots are nearest to the house. Their trunks are marked with a white spray-painted X like they've got the plague or something. I've almost reached the gate when I see what's been left on the gatepost.

It's my bobble hat, covered in dew. Someone must've found it. It's been folded up very neatly and turned inside out.

I can't help grinning. So Borage didn't maul my hat to death after all. Perhaps it's a sign the day's getting better. Shaking off the dew, I turn my hat back the right way again and put it on. Then I go through the gate.

I remember this bit of the path. It starts off narrow, then disappears completely. Borage charges along, dragging me behind him. It's not exactly fun. These aren't tidy woods like the ones near home with a cinder path running through the middle. We used to go there on a Sunday sometimes, back when Theo could still ride his bike.

Darkling Wood is messy, full of dead leaves and brambles. It's easy to imagine tree roots pushing through the soil. Growing and growing toward the house and nothing being able to stop them. No wonder Nell wants the trees cut down.

We come out into a clearing. Without leaves, the trees go up and up until they almost curve over and touch each other. The air feels damp and heavy like a wet cloth across my face. I pull my hat down over my ears, shivering. Borage might've snatched it off my head in the first place, but dogs don't return things by leaving them neatly folded on gateposts.

Someone was here last night. In the woods.

A sudden gust of wind makes the trees creak. Borage freezes. His back fur sticks up like he's sensed something. I wrap his lead around my wrist, bracing myself. There's no sign of anything. Or anyone. Borage relaxes. As he starts sniffing again, my heartbeat begins to slow. I'm surprised at how jumpy I am.

I feel better once I've left the woods behind me and am out in the open fields. The sun is shining. It's a pretty nice day for November. To my right, at the bottom of the valley, is a church and some gray stone houses; Borage heads for them like he knows where he's going, dragging me behind him down the hill. We end up in the village square, which is where the shop is. It's got a tatty striped awning at the front and a hook to tie up your dog.

I'm barely through the door when the man behind the counter says, "You'll be Nell Campbell's granddaughter, then?"

Wow, I think. News travels fast.

There's one other customer, a man in filthy wellies, who stares at me almost without blinking.

"Um . . . yes . . ." I try to smile. Neither of them smiles back.

"When's them trees of hers coming down?" says the counter man, arms folded. "She's got root trouble, so I heard. That wood's growing too close to the house."

"She has," I say. "I mean . . . it is."

"That still don't make it right to cut 'em down," says the other man. "Been there longer than she has, them trees. She can't just hack down what doesn't suit her."

The counter man nods. "People around here aren't happy

about what she's planning, you know—not that the council gives a monkey's. But the villagers do."

He stares at me like somehow it's my fault. I don't know what to say. Grabbing what I need for cheese and beetroot sandwiches, I hand over Nell's money and say goodbye. I'm glad to get back outside again.

"What was that about, eh?" I say to Borage. He twitches his ears to show he's listening. Shame he can't answer, as it's pretty obvious Nell's not popular around here.

We start the long climb out of the village. This hill's so steep, I have to stop to catch my breath, and as I do my phone starts ringing. It's Lexie. In a flash, I dump the bag of shopping and dig into my pocket for my phone.

"Hey you," she says.

It's so nice to hear her voice.

"Hey! Are you a big sister yet?"

"No. False alarm. That baby's got Mum's timekeeping abilities, I swear."

I grin down the phone. "Poor Kate!"

Lexie's got two mums—Kate, her real mum, who's late for everything, and Jen, her mum's partner.

"Is it break time now?" I imagine a normal school day, with boring lessons and then homework, and think how much I'd rather be there than stuck here.

"Yup. Just had PE. Double Maths is next." Then she shouts to someone in the background, "I'm taking them off!"

I picture Lexie in the school changing rooms, undoing her football cleats. She hates maths, but she's really, *really* good at football. She doesn't brag about it either, not like a boy would.

"How was PE?" I ask.

"Good," she says. "Listen, I'm so sad you couldn't come to ours."

"Me too."

"How's Theo?"

"All right, I think. Mum's not said much."

"That makes a change!"

I try to laugh, but Lexie's right: it's not like Mum to hold back.

"Are you okay?" she says.

I look down at my shopping. Some of it has tumbled out onto the road.

"I'm fine," I say.

"What about your grandma? What's it like there?"

"She's odd."

Lexie giggles.

"D'you miss me?" I say.

"Course I miss you. I'm having to sit next to Bethany Cox all week."

In the background, a teacher tells Lexie to put her phone away because break time's over.

"I'll text you," she says. The teacher speaks again.

"You'd better go."

We say goodbye and hang up. I follow the road until I see the same field and the same stile I climbed earlier. My head's full of home. Talking to Lexie hasn't really helped; it's just made me miss it even more.

When I'm back in the woods, Borage starts pulling. His back hair has gone bristly again.

I tug on the lead. "Calm down, mister!"

But try as I might, I can't hold him, not with my right arm

being yanked from its socket. I have to let go of the lead. He's gone within seconds. Convincing myself he's heading in the direction of the house, I set off after him. I just pray Nell doesn't find him first.

The woods are silent in that eerie way classrooms are after school has ended. I walk faster.

Then, behind me, something rustles. Thinking it's Borage, I spin around.

Just a few feet away is a girl in a red coat, frozen to the spot. She's staring right at me. I stare back. We stay like that for one long second. Then she runs away, through the trees, before I can even say hello.

6

To my massive relief, I find Borage sitting on the back doorstep. Once inside, he heads straight to the room Nell calls the library and presses his nose up against the door: I suppose this means she's in there. I should probably wait till she comes out again, but I want to ask her about the village and the girl I've just seen, so I make her a cup of coffee and take it in.

She's sitting at a desk over by the window, sifting through piles of paperwork. A little electric heater hums away at her feet but the room is still freezing. It's dark in here too, despite the big bay window. Borage settles down next to her chair.

"Here," I say, offering her the steaming cup.

She looks surprised. But, with the tiniest nod, she takes it and wraps her hands around it.

"You made it back, I see," she says. "The locals didn't eat you up." She says it with a wry smile so I guess she already knows what they think of her in Bexton.

"They weren't exactly welcoming at the shop," I say.

"No, they wouldn't be. I'm not very popular in Bexton these

days. So much fuss about a bunch of old trees. The sooner my wood comes down the better."

"When is it happening?"

She looks down at her desk. It's a mass of papers—bills, letters, maps with colored lines on them and the words "Land Registry" at the top.

"That, my dear, is a good question. The council say there's no preservation order on any of the trees, and because they're potentially dangerous, you see, they've given it the go-ahead."

"So why the delay?"

"I've not yet found a single tree surgeon who is willing to do the job. I've tried all the local numbers and a few further afield. No one wants to cut down my wood."

"Why's that?"

Nell shrugs. "It's an old wood. People around here like their countryside untouched. They don't want change. Word's got about that I'm a bad person for wanting rid of the trees. And bingo—I'm the local villain."

She doesn't seem overly bothered. I'm not sure if I admire her or feel sorry for her.

"But you said the roots were growing too close to the house and it wasn't safe. And that you wanted more light in your garden. That sounds fair enough," I say.

She blinks. Takes a sip of coffee.

"Yes," she says. "So I'll keep trying until I find someone to do it."

Reaching down to stroke Borage, she stares out the window. The view looks over the lawn to those trees marked with white crosses. Not all the trees are the same type. Some look like the ones in our park back home, others are tall and spindly.

All of them are bare because it's winter. They make me think of skinny fingers reaching toward the house.

"Beastly things, aren't they?" Nell says, meaning the trees.

I think of the rustlings I heard out there last night.

"They're kind of creepy."

"Creepy?" Nell snorts.

She obviously doesn't think so. But I'm sure someone *was* in the woods last night. And today I found my folded-up hat—placed there by . . . who? That girl I've just seen?

"Do any young people live around here?" I ask.

"What sort of young people?"

"I came across a girl in the woods. She ran off before I could speak to her."

Nell tuts. "Travelers, I shouldn't wonder. Probably one of that lot camped out up at Glossop's Farm."

"Is that near here?"

"About a mile that way." She points in the opposite direction to the village. "The house is derelict, the fields are all rented out. When the Travelers arrived a few months ago and set up camp, the council tried to move them on. But they've not managed it yet."

"Oh."

So the girl in the red coat is probably a Traveler who lives nearby. Yet it doesn't explain why anyone would be in Darkling Wood in the middle of the night. Was it her, or someone else? It's a bit odd. But then, I suppose *I* was out there too.

"Next time you see that Traveler girl, let me know," says Nell. "My wood is private property; she clearly needs to be reminded of that fact."

I look at Nell sideways. She's got a fierce face. Strong nose, big jaw. Dad's gray eyes. I bet she was beautiful once. Now, though, she's spiky like the trees.

"Do you think the girl will come back, then?" I ask.

Before Nell can answer, the phone rings out in the hall.

"I'll go!"

Please let it be Mum saying she'll come and take me home.

"Hello?" I say.

"Alice?"

"Mum!" I sink into the chair next to the telephone table.

"Don't get too excited." She sounds serious. Something's not right.

"The doctor's just been to see us," she says. "Theo's temperature is a bit too high, so they're giving him antibiotics."

"Oh." My stomach drops. "He's got an infection?"

"Just a little one. The doctor says they're quite common in transplant patients. So once the antibiotics get to work, he'll be fine. It's nothing to worry about, really."

This is more like Mum, making it sound like it's no big deal.

"Can I come and see him?" I ask. "I did promise. And I've done him a card."

There's a very long pause. "Give it a few days, love." In the meantime, I'm stuck here and Mum and Theo are there. I twist the phone cord tight around my finger.

"Are you okay?" Mum says.

I'm not. She's not either—I can hear the strain in her voice. And I can't *do* anything. I take a deep breath.

"Are you sure this infection isn't bad? Only in the booklet it says . . ."

Mum interrupts. "He'll be fine. Now please, stop worrying, will you? It doesn't help."

I grit my teeth. All the time I'm just stuck here, waiting for the phone to ring. It's doing my head in. There must be some way I can help.

"Alice? Are you still there?" Mum says.

"Yes."

"Listen, this infection has set things back a few days. So I need you to understand, and be okay with it."

I guess the next bit. "Which means I'll have to stay here longer."

The kid part of me wants to scream "IT'S NOT FAIR!" But what's the point? None of this is fair. So I swallow it and say goodbye.

As soon as I'm off the phone, Nell's in the hallway. I'm not sure how long she's been listening.

"It's school for you if you're staying on," Nell says. "We can't have you lounging around here all day." She isn't serious. *Is she?*

"But I've brought schoolwork with me. I've got loads to do," I say.

She raises her eyebrows. "There's a school in the next town. I'll make inquiries. It'll do you good."

"No it won't," I tell her. The thought of facing a class full of strangers makes me feel ill. Today at the shop was bad enough.

Nell refuses to have any of it.

"When sorrows come, young lady, they come not as single spies but in battalions."

If that's meant to make me feel better, it doesn't. Nor does the fact that Nell hasn't even asked how her sick grandson is.

7

After lunch, I'm at the sink washing up when Borage slopes inside. He looks like he's just had a telling-off, which is odd considering how Nell dotes on him.

I go to the back doorstep. "What's he done wrong?" Nell's holding her garden fork like a weapon. "*He's* done nothing. But, look, someone has." She points at the trees nearest the fence.

I can't see anything unusual. There's just the fence and beyond it, the first of the trees.

"That girl you saw in the woods, I bet this was *her* doing," Nell says.

Now I'm interested. I join her outside and see what she's staring at. The trees that were marked this morning are now . . . well . . . *not.*

"The white crosses have come off," I say.

"Indeed, my dear."

"How? I mean, it hasn't rained." Not that spray paint comes off in the rain; at least, it didn't when Lexie and I did our bikes with it last summer.

"It's a trick, Alice, that's what it is," she says. "People are against me cutting down Darkling Wood—the Travelers, the villagers, everyone. And now *someone* has done this on purpose to scare me off. It's vandalism!"

I don't think it's worked.

"Right," Nell says. "Let's see if your friend is still in the woods, shall we?"

"She's not my friend!"

But Nell's already striding off across the lawn. This is so embarrassing. She's about to lay into a girl who probably goes to the local school, the one I've got to go to any day now.

Then, by some miracle, we hear the telephone ring. Nell stops. She thrusts her garden fork into the ground.

"Drat. I'd better answer that. It might be a tree surgeon," she says. "Have a look for that girl, will you?" As she goes inside, I head for the spot where I saw the girl this morning. There's no sign of anyone. Everything's covered in heavy dew that might actually be frost. It's cold. A damp, raw cold that gets in your bones. I wish I'd worn my coat and hat.

Shivering, I pull out my phone. There's one measly signal bar but no missed calls or texts from Lexie, so I stuff it back in my pocket and keep walking.

"You've not brought the dog, have you?" says a nearby voice.

I stop dead.

"Only I'm afraid of dogs."

I can't see anyone, just trees.

"I'm up here," says the voice, a girl's.

I look up. Dangling inches from my head are a pair of boots. They're so close I can see their muddy soles. It makes me jump.

"Blimey!" I say. "Do you always sneak up on people?"

The girl is sitting right above me in a tree. It's the same girl from this morning; I recognize her red coat. As she looks down at me, her hair falls forward. It's very long and honey-colored, and full of knots.

"Promise me there's no dog," she says again.

I feel a flurry of excitement. "The dog's not here, honest. He's inside in his bed."

"Watch out, then," she says. "I'm coming down." She lands nearby with a thud.

"Ouch, that was further than I thought," she says, shaking out her feet.

I open my mouth to speak. I need to tell her what Nell said, that this is private property and she's trespassing. But I can't stop staring. She looks about my age, only smaller than me. And she's wearing the weirdest outfit. Her boots make me think of ice skates without the blades, and she's got on what looks like a petticoat. Over the top of it, her red coat reaches almost to the ground.

Finally, I get my words out. "Is that why you ran off earlier? Because of the dog?"

She nods, pushing her hair off her face. She's pretty in a pink-cheeked, blue-eyed sort of way that reminds me of a china doll.

"I'm sorry, you must have thought me very rude," she says.

Very odd, more like.

"But, you see, there is a reason I don't like dogs."

"Did you get bitten or something?" I ask.

"Yes, and it went poisonous. I was very sick."

"Didn't you take antibiotics?" She looks at me blankly.

"Tablets. They get rid of the infection," I say, thinking suddenly about Theo.

Still the blank look. Perhaps I know too much about medicine for a person my age.

Then she wipes her hand in her coat and holds it out to me. "Let's do this properly: I'm Flo, short for Florence. Named after my great-great-grandmother. How do you do?"

No one at my school would dream of introducing themselves like that. Or of shaking hands.

"I'm Alice," I say. "I've no idea who I'm named after." I don't take her hand; it's easier not to when she's being nice and I've got to ask her to leave.

"Look, my grandmother thinks you wiped the crosses off her trees," I say. "She's furious. And if she catches you here she'll—"

Flo interrupts. "She thinks it's *me*?"

"Yes, and you'd better not come back here at night, either. She hasn't said so, but I reckon if she catches you again she'll call the police." I add this bit just to warn Flo. I don't want her getting in trouble. "Thanks for finding my hat, though."

"Hat? What hat?"

"The one you left on the gatepost. You'd turned it inside out."

"Aha," she says, like something's just occurred to her. "You think that was me too?"

"Wasn't it?"

She beckons to me. "Come."

Flo sets off in a direction I've not walked in before, going so fast it's difficult to keep up. The path dips and winds between the bushes until we end up in front of a very large tree.

"This is a beech tree," says Flo. Her hand rests on the trunk. "It's very special because of its magical properties. Do you know, you can sometimes see fairies here?"

It's hard to keep a straight face.

"Fairies? Are you serious?"

"Yes, fairies," she says, quite matter-of-fact. "The hidden people. They're all around us. Darkling Wood is full of them."

I try not to laugh.

"I'm sorry. ... It's just that ..." The words *mad, bonkers, ridiculous* are about to burst from my mouth.

"You don't believe me," says Flo.

"No offense," I say, "but no one actually *believes* in fairies."

Flo looks at me as if I'm the one who's mad. "Let me tell you, it was the fairies who wiped the crosses off those trees. They found your hat too, and turned it inside out. They're trying to tell you something."

"What d'you mean?"

"Those are just warnings, Alice—tricks to get your attention. The woods are the fairies' home and if your grandmother goes ahead with cutting them down, there'll be no more warnings. No more tricks. It'll be out-and-out revenge."

I sigh. This is getting stupid.

"Look, the trees aren't safe," I say. "They're growing too close to the cottage, that's all I know. Nell's only protecting what's hers."

"That won't count for anything if she upsets the fairies. Be warned: if she goes ahead, they will take their revenge. And it'll be far worse than anything they've done so far."

She is joking. She must be.

She's staring over my shoulder now. I turn to see what she's looking at. There's movement in the bushes. I hear her gasp. For one stupid second I wonder if she really *has* seen a fairy.

But what's caught her attention is the gray blur streaking toward us.

"Borage, stop!" I cry, blocking the path.

As he skids to a very clumsy halt, I grab his collar.

"He looks scary, but he's all right, really," I say, turning to Flo. There is no Flo. She's vanished.

Darkling Cottage
Tuesday, 12 November, 1918

My dear Alfred,

Apologies for the tiny writing—it's a job to get my hands on any paper with everything being in such short supply. I've much to tell you. The queerest thing happened today, and because you're a real brick you might just believe me. Be warned though, it is completely MAD.

I'll start from the beginning.

Dear Maisie took ill at lunchtime. She was serving the potatoes when all of a sudden she had to sit down. Sweat broke off her as if she'd been out in the rain, so Mama sent her to bed and called Dr. Wyatt, who says it's influenza.

As if that wasn't awful enough, I was then instructed to do her afternoon chores. It's not funny, Alfred, not in the slightest. After a good telling-off about "my responsibilities to this household" (I won't repeat it, but it wasn't pleasant or fair), Mama sent me to the village with a basket and her ration book.

In the queue outside the shop the talk was of 'flu and which boys were home from the Front. There were black armbands everywhere I looked. It wasn't very cheering, let me tell you. Nor was coming home with such small parcels of food. There wasn't nearly enough bacon for your stomach, dear brother. And to see our butter done up in such a tiny bundle made me want to weep.

As usual, I took the path through the wood. I'd nearly reached our gate when I saw the oddest, queerest thing. One moment, the path was clear. Then two people appeared around the corner. I say "people," for they were human-shaped and appeared to be dancing. Yet the only music I heard was birdsong.

Stranger than any of this, though, was their size. They were TINY. Don't think me mad when I tell you they were the height of a milk jug. It's hard to believe, but imagine it, Alfred, a person not more than a few inches tall and dressed entirely in green! Stranger still, something fine like silk seemed to flutter between their shoulder blades, which I can only describe as wings.

In my shock, I dropped the basket. The "people" took fright and vanished. Did they run, or fly? I couldn't tell you. Where they had been, the air seemed to ripple, like the surface of a pond after a stone is thrown into it.

As I picked up the basket again, it felt heavier. By the time I reached home my arm was aching, and as I handed the groceries over to Mrs. Cotter, she positively beamed. She'd never seen so much bacon, so she said. And hadn't they been kind with the butter this week?

I confess I was very perplexed. The parcels I'd purchased had been meager things, yet now they looked very decent-sized indeed. It was as if a magic spell or some such thing had been cast on them.

Now you know me and secrets: I really couldn't keep this to myself. But without you here, I was a bit stuck as for who to tell. Finding Mama and Papa in the library, I'm afraid I blurted everything out to them.

Papa lowered his book and said did I know I was born

between midnight on Friday and dawn on Saturday, which meant I was a Chime Child? According to old folklore, it meant I could see fairies and spirits.

Now this wasn't the reaction I'd expected, and I rather liked the idea. Until Papa's moustache twitched, that is, and I saw he was only teasing. Then came the part I did expect. Mama lectured me about how I already spend unhealthy amounts of time in the woods; I didn't need my head filling with Papa's silly stories.

I didn't care to hear any of this. In fact, it made me feel rather out of sorts. So when Mama asked if I was all right, I admitted I had a headache coming on—I'd not noticed until then. She reached over and felt my forehead, declaring it burning hot.

So here I am, propped up on pillows writing to you. Chime Child or not, my head is pounding. Every part of me aches, even my fingernails and toenails, if that's possible. Poor Maisie has my absolute sympathy: this 'flu is ghastly.

Yet do believe me when I tell you what I saw today. It wasn't fever or my wild imagination, though our parents believe it was both. I'm desperate to see those winged "people" again. And I want you to see them, Alfred, for they were something otherworldly, of that I'm certain.

Until then,
Your dearest sister

8

Wednesday, 13 November

It turns out the local school can take me straightaway. So just after eight o'clock, Nell drives me up to the main road, where I'll catch the bus for Ferndean High School. I'm a bag of nerves, and Nell's mood isn't helping. A man was supposed to come today to start work on the wood, but he's canceled, so Nell's driving like a maniac, and by the time I get out of the car, I'm feeling sick.

Two girls are at the bus stop already. Neither of them is Flo, though I'm guessing she must go to Ferndean High because it's the only secondary school for miles. The girls are listening to music, sharing the headphones and singing badly like me and Lexie do. It makes me miss my best friend even more.

The headphone girls notice me watching. They nudge each other. I try to smile. Like the men in the shop, they don't smile back. My stomach sinks. *Please don't let it be like this all day.*

After another few minutes, the school bus arrives. Inside it's already so rammed the windows have steamed up. The headphone girls sit with their mates who've saved them seats. I hang on to the tiny hope that Flo's already on board, and when she sees me she'll ask me to sit with her. But there's no girl in a red coat here. There are no free seats either. People are staring now. I feel my cheeks getting warm.

"Didn't know I had an extra one today. You're new, are you?" says the driver.

I nod. Everyone else is in blazers and ties. And here's me in jeans and sneakers because it's all I've brought from home. The driver reaches behind him. He pulls down a foldout seat.

"Sit here for today," he says. "And put your belt on." The seat is at right angles to everyone else's, which means I'm in full view of the whole bus.

Great, I think gritting my teeth, just *great*.

Things don't improve massively when I get to school. In reception a bald-headed man in a tight, shiny suit introduces himself as Mr. Jennings, my Head of Year. He gives me a printout of my timetable.

"Period one is history," he says. "Come on, I'll walk you over."

First, though, he takes me to Lost Property. The cupboard is so big we both stand inside it, which is horrible because it stinks of old PE clothes. Plastic boxes labeled "coats," "school skirts," "black shoes" are on every shelf. Mr. Jennings reaches into one and pulls out a blazer.

"Try this."

I hold it between my fingers.

"It won't bite," Mr. Jennings says.

He also gives me a tie, a shirt, and a skirt, which I'm to wear tomorrow. It all smells of someone else. When I get back to Nell's I'll have to wash the lot, but for now I stuff it into my bag.

The history block is on the other side of the school. We go down corridors, up stairs, across these funny walkways that link different buildings. The whole place looks like it's grown over the years, so there's extra brick bits, glass bits, even a few of those ugly gray huts. It's nothing like my old school, which is sleek and new and looks like a supermarket.

"You're staying at Darkling Cottage, eh?" Mr. Jennings says. "Interesting place your grandmother's got there."

He's doing the friendly teacher thing and I suppose it beats making small talk about heart transplants, but only just. I bet he knows what's happening to the wood. And I bet he's got an opinion about it too. But he moves on, telling me my lesson "buddies" for the next few weeks will be Max and Ella.

"They're great students," he says. "You'll probably find you've lots in common."

All I hear is the word *weeks*.

The class is working quietly when we arrive. As the door opens, everyone looks up. Thirty pairs of eyes fix on me. I feel my palms go damp and just hope no one here wants to shake hands like Flo did.

Mr. Jennings leaves, and the class teacher directs me to a free seat. I'm glad to sit down. There's a boy on one side of me; on the other side is a girl wearing badges on her blazer.

"I'm Ella," she whispers. I try to smile.

"That's Max." She points her pen at the boy next to me, who gives a lazy wave.

I'm passed an exercise book and told to put my name on it. The teacher says her name is Mrs. Copeland, and before I've even got my pencil case out, the lesson picks up again. With everyone watching the teacher now, I sneak a quick look around for Flo, but there's no sign of her. She must be in another class.

On the wall there's a display about the First World War, with old photos and newspaper stories. One picture is of lines and lines of war graves stretching away over the hill into the distance; I can't believe there's so many. It's not like I knew those men or anything, but they were someone's dad, someone's brother. It makes me get a lump in my throat.

Meanwhile, Mrs. Copeland is still talking.

"... so our next class project will follow directly. We'll be exploring the impact of the First World War on normal people's lives, what happened *after* the war ended. For your projects, I'd like you each to choose a person who was alive in 1918. No one famous, please—just everyday, normal people. Your focus will be to find out how the end of the war affected their life."

There's groaning in the back row, which Mrs. Copeland bats away with her hand.

"Honestly," she says. "I set you lot an interesting topic, and you'd think I'd asked you to remove your own toenails!"

To be honest, the project sounds better than the Romans, which is what we were doing back home. Ella thinks so too; she's already got an idea for hers and it's to do with animals.

"Surprise, surprise," says Max, rolling his eyes.

"Animals were affected by the war," she says. "People always forget that."

"But the project is meant to be about a *person*," says Max.

"So?" Ella shrugs. "It can be a *person* who works with animals, can't it?"

One of the badges on Ella's blazer says "Rats Have Rights." The others are of dolphins and elephants. Max sees I've noticed.

"She's an animal activist, aren't you, Ella?" he says, and grins at me. I grin back.

"The word is *conservationist,* stupid," she says, but looks pleased.

"Better not tell her where you're staying, Alice, or what your gran's about to do to those trees of hers," Max says.

I stop grinning. These people are such gossips.

Is there anyone who actually *doesn't* know about Darkling Wood? I stare at my exercise book, wishing we could talk about something else, but Ella's now trying to read my face.

"What's that about trees?" She's frowning. Thinking. Then she slaps the table. "Not Darkling Wood? Are you staying there? *Really?*"

She says it so sharply the students in front of us turn and stare. I squirm in my seat.

"Yes, but only for a bit," I say.

"So your grandmother's the one who wants to cut down the wood?"

"She says she has to. The trees are growing too close to the house and it's unsafe."

Ella pulls a face and goes quiet. I don't think she believes me. When the lesson ends, she doesn't wait for me, either. She's been told to be my class buddy, but she clearly doesn't want to be my friend.

9

The after-school bus drops me in the village square. Walking the steep hill home, I get my phone out. There are no messages from Mum or Lexie, but that single bar of reception makes me call them both because I'm dying to talk to someone from home. When neither of them answers, my eyes fill up, although I'd probably cry if they'd answered too; it's been that sort of day.

Reaching the woods, I walk slowly, kicking up leaves. The air smells muddy and damp. All I hear now is the wind in the treetops. It's a whooshing, roaring sound like you get inside a seashell, even when you're a million miles from the sea.

Everything *is* far away, that's the problem. I've never gone this long without Mum or Theo. All day they've kept popping into my head. I'd be doing fractions or thinking Max had a nice smile or wondering why Ella was in a sulk, and then—*ouch*—I'd remember: I'm here—they're there. Though it's a different sort of hurt from when Dad left for Devon, because then he chose to go.

Out of the gloom, something red comes toward me. It's Flo. I'm stupidly pleased.

"You got here quick!" I say, grinning. "D'you catch a different school bus or something?"

"Stop!" she cries. "Don't come any closer!"

"What?"

"Stay where you are! Don't move!"

Her hands are in the air, palms facing me. She looks panicked. I feel the grin freezing on my face.

"Now," she says, taking a deep breath. "Very slowly take a step back."

"But . . ."

"Just do it, Alice!"

"All right! Keep your hair on!" I do as I'm told.

"Now take another step, and another, until you're back by that tree." She points to an old twisted trunk. Once I'm standing by it, she comes over—not directly, but in a roundabout way like she's avoiding a certain spot.

"It's a good job you didn't step inside the ring!" she says, pink-cheeked and flustered. "That almost went *horribly* wrong!"

I've not the foggiest what she's on about.

"The fairy ring," she says. "Didn't you see it?"

She's pointing to the place where, moments ago, I'd been about to step. All I see is dead leaves. *Nothing odd in that.* The entire floor of this wood is covered in the same carpet of reds and yellows and browns.

"It's late in the season, but you can see where mushrooms were," she says. "Look. Here. And here."

She traces a circle shape with her finger. I don't know about the fairy part, but there's certainly some stubby gray things poking up through the leaves.

"Go on, then, what would've happened if I'd stepped into the fairy ring?" I ask.

I'm thinking thunder. Lightning. Or nothing at all. It's very hard to keep a straight face, especially as Flo looks so serious.

"You'd become invisible," she says. "Or the fairies would make you dance until you died."

"Right, *of course.*" This is nuts. Then she points at my bobble hat, which I'm wearing pulled right down over my ears.

"But if you'd worn your hat inside out, it would've protected you."

She's back on that again.

"Wow. That's . . . um . . . helpful to know, thanks," I say.

Irritably, she stuffs her hands in her pockets. "I wish you'd believe me. This is terribly important, you know."

"Sorry."

I don't want to upset her. The thing is, I'm glad Flo's here. She's, I don't know, *different.* I wonder if she wears that red coat to school; it'd stand out a mile. But then if she's a Traveler, she might not go to school, and maybe that's why I didn't see her today.

"Do you care for these woods?" says Flo suddenly. I'm caught off guard. *Care?* It's an odd thing to ask.

"They're kind of beautiful, in an eerie way," I say. "But I get why Nell wants them cut down. The roots growing so close to the house means she'll end up with subsidence. . . ."

"What?"

"It's something to do with the foundations of the house becoming unsafe. . . ."

"I know what it *means*," Flo snaps. "And it's clear what your grandmother feels about Darkling Wood. But I asked what *you* think of it. Do *you* care?"

49

Do I? It's not something I've really thought about. Looking at the trees, they seem less spooky today.

More mysterious. As I take a deep breath, I feel something, though I'm not sure what it is.

Flo speaks first. "Your grandmother plans to clear this wood, and in doing so will destroy the homes of the fairies that live here. It's a terrible, pointless thing she wants to do."

"It's not pointless to her," I say, feeling like I'm defending Nell. "Darkling Cottage is her home and she doesn't want it falling down around her. It's *her* home she's worried about. And she wants to let more light in because the house is really dark inside. Honestly, we've always got the lights on."

"So you believe her?"

"Why wouldn't I?"

Flo's mouth tightens. "I see. But you don't believe me."

She's right, of course; I don't believe her. But there's a big difference between pretending there are fairies and wanting your house to be safe. Yet I don't want her to hate me because of Nell. I had a taste of that from Ella at school today and it didn't feel very nice.

"Go on, then, explain it to me," I say. "Why should I believe in fairies?"

Flo squares her shoulders.

"The fairies are trying to save Darkling Wood because it's their home. They're using their magic to delay things, to cause upsets—mischief, if you like—so that your grandmother will get fed up and abandon her plans."

It sounds like a story. Or a film. It certainly doesn't sound real.

"You want me to believe this?"

"If you do, it'll make their magic more powerful, more likely to succeed."

"I don't see how."

Flo pushes her hair off her face and fixes me with her very blue eyes.

"Think of your home," she says. There's a break in her voice now. It tugs at something in me. "Think of what it means to you."

I don't need to think. I know.

My home is the ache in my chest, and though I'm trying hard not to let it, it's eating away at me. It's the thing that's missing. It's our house, Number 24 Eastbourne Terrace with blue and red glass in the front door so that when the sun shines through it, it makes colored patches on the floor.

And I miss it I miss it I miss it.

Flo keeps talking. "This wood belongs to the fairies. It's *their* home. We can't just take things that don't belong to us. I've learned that the hard way, believe me. So, Alice, I'm asking you to open your mind, to believe that something magical does exist here in Darkling Wood. If you do, it'll give the fairies strength to save the trees."

"Why me? Why does what I think matter?"

"There are reasons," Flo says.

I frown. "Like what?"

"I don't know," she says. "But the fairies have picked you—that's why they turned your hat inside out."

I still don't believe her. It's all too bizarre. Too weird. And yet I'm aware of a stillness coming over me. I feel calm and peaceful. I haven't felt like this in days.

Then, up ahead, I hear the gate click. People are coming;

their voices get nearer. One of the speakers is Nell. My heart thumps. She's not going to be thrilled to find me here with Flo, not after the white crosses got wiped off and I was meant to warn her about trespassing.

"Get down!" I hiss to Flo. "She mustn't see you!"

We crouch behind a clump of bracken. Fingers crossed it's enough to hide Flo's coat. The speakers come into view now. Nell is with a man who's wearing one of those fluorescent jackets, and as she points at the trees, he scribbles things down in a notebook. I hold my breath. They're standing near the fairy ring. Another step and they'll be inside it, and for a split second I think about warning them, though of what, exactly?

I bite my lip. My heart keeps thudding, not from nerves now but something else.

I sense Flo watching me.

"What?" I mouth.

She gives me a tiny smile. "You feel it too, don't you? You know there's magic in these woods."

I'm not sure what I'm feeling, but as I look at Nell and the man, my fists seem to clench up tight.

"I knew I could count on you, Alice," Flo whispers.

I don't know what to think, but it seems we're friends now, which is a start, at least.

10

"How was school today?" Nell asks at supper.

I'm relieved that's *all* she's asking. It would've been worse—much worse—if she'd caught Flo and me hiding in the woods.

"Did you make any friends?"

"Not really."

"Why was that, dear?"

I hesitate. But she's in a good mood so I tell her.

"People in my class seem to know about the woods."

"And?"

I fiddle with my fork. "It's like they're judging me because of it."

"The eco-warrior bunch, eh?"

Her cheerfulness is down to that man in the fluorescent jacket, who apparently is a tree surgeon she hopes will do the job. I think of what Flo said about home, and how peaceful it felt out there under the trees this afternoon. Maybe there *is* magic in Darkling Wood—not fairies, but *something*. Perhaps it isn't right to destroy the whole wood. There might be some other way.

"What's the matter?" says Nell. "You're scowling."

"Just thinking," I say, and turn away to get plates down off the dresser.

The microwave pings. As Nell opens the door to take out a plastic container of bubbling white gloop, my stomach heaves. I can't face much more of her cooking.

After forcing down supper, my next challenge is tonight's homework, which is maths and some verbs to learn for French. Nell's shut herself in the library, so I spread my books out over the kitchen table. Tucked in my old school planner I find the card I made for Theo. It's looking tatty; the edges are curling and there's a candy wrapper stuck to the back. A decent sister would've sent it by now. It's no good to anyone stuffed inside my bag.

I can't concentrate on homework tonight, so, putting it to one side, I get my borrowed school uniform out to wash. Except the washing machine is so old I can't make it work, so I fill the sink with hot water and do everything by hand. Borage watches from his bed. Just as I'm draping things around the stove to dry, the phone rings.

"Don't touch," I warn him as I run to answer it. Nell gets there first like she's expecting a call.

"It's your mother," she says, handing me the phone.

"Hi, sweetie, how was today?"

Mum sounds cheerful. I'm so glad to hear her that my eyes go misty.

"It was all right," I say. "What about Theo?"

"Have you got to wear the uniform? What color is it? Don't tell me it's dark green—we had to wear that at my old school and it was . . ."

"MUM!" She stops.

"How *is* he? Is the infection clearing up? When can I see him? When can I come home?" There's a pause.

"I've done him a card," I say.

Mum sighs. "You are sweet. I'm sure you can visit him soon."

"And Dad? Does he know how Theo is?"

"I've spoken to him now, yes."

"Is he coming to the hospital?"

"I don't know. Apparently the baby's teething, so . . ." She trails off.

Excuses. More excuses.

"So," says Mum, still trying to sound cheerful. "Tell me about your grandma. What's the house like?"

"You must have been here—before you had us, I mean."

"No, never, though I met Nell a couple of times when you were very young."

"And was she . . . I don't know . . . so *spiky* back then?"

Mum laughs. "She's quite formidable, if that's what you mean. But underneath it all she's got a good heart. I'm sorry we lost touch with her when you were growing up."

"Why did we?"

"Your father," says Mum, serious now. "He didn't ever want to see her, and he never wanted to go back to the house—don't ask me why. I tried asking, but he wouldn't talk about it. It was always like shutters coming down."

I glance at the library door. It's closed, but I still drop my voice.

"It *is* a bit odd here, Mum. There's these woods around the house and Nell wants them cut down. . . ."

I stop. Something gray lopes past me carrying a yellow-and-black tie.

"Stupid dog's got my school tie! I can't believe it!" I cry.

Mum giggles.

"It's not even funny," I say. "I've got to wear that tie tomorrow."

"Oh Alice, he probably only wants to play."

Which makes my chest ache for Theo because it's just the sort of stupid trick he'd pull, and a dog is no substitute for a brother.

"Go and get your tie back," says Mum. "I'll call you tomorrow."

"Okay. Kiss Theo for me."

Putting the phone down, I sprint after Borage. He won't have gone up to the attic because he hates the narrow staircase, but I can't see him on the first floor either.

At the top of the stairs is the bathroom. Turn left and a long passage runs past all the bedrooms. I've never been down it; I don't know why, but it gives me the creeps—something about those closed doors and how dark the passage is. It makes the walls and ceiling feel too close.

Once the lights are on, I count seven closed doors. It's a lot of bedrooms; I suppose once upon a time one of them was Dad's. There's no sign of Borage anywhere. The first room on my left is Nell's. I don't want to go in, not without asking, so I peep quickly around the door.

No Borage.

The next room is empty but for a bed and a box of books. I suppose it could've been a boy's room once, but now it smells of damp, like no one's been in here for years.

Opposite this room, the wall curves and there are two steps down to a doorway that's hidden behind a red curtain. I'm about to look there next when my phone beeps. My phone *actually* beeps! I can't believe it. I whip it out of my pocket and see a text from Lexie.

Got your message. How's the new school? Soooo boring without you. Miss you heaps xxx

If I go back up the steps, there's a bar of signal right here in the passageway. I dial Lexie's number. She picks up after three rings.

"Hey!" I say. "You're not doing homework, are you?"

"Done it," she says. "How's Theo? What's the latest?"

"Quite poorly still," I say, though with Mum being so cagey I'm not totally sure. "What about you? Got a brother or sister yet?"

"Nope. I'm starting to think it's just a cushion up Mum's jumper."

"You wait," I say. "Once you change a nappy, you'll see it's no cushion."

Lexie giggles. It makes me giggle too. Then she says, "Bethany Cox has asked me to a sleepover at her house." I stop laughing. "Why would I want to go? All they do is talk about makeup."

"Have you said no, then?"

Lexie pauses. "Not yet. Can't see me going, though, can you?"

I start to feel nasty inside. Actually, I *can* see Lexie at Bethany's house. Not the toenail-painting bit or trying on clothes. But there'll be pizza and films and other people from school; she'll have a great time.

"You've gone quiet, Al," Lexie says.

I sigh. "I missed you today, that's all. The new school's a bit rubbish and now the dog's run off with my tie and I can't find him—or it."

"Want to talk about the rubbish stuff?"

"Not really."

"So let's find this tie-eating dog," says Lexie. "Where've you already looked?"

"Down the corridor. In a couple of the rooms."

"Try another room."

The curtained-off door is right here. I go back down the steps. It's dark enough to make my phone light up. The curtain's stiff with dust as I lift it. The door handle underneath won't move. Tucking the phone under my chin, I lean into the door with my shoulder, but it doesn't budge.

"It's locked."

"I bet the dog's locked himself in there," laughs Lexie. I giggle. Then stop.

"Shhh!" I say. "Someone's coming."

I hear footsteps, then a creak in the floorboards. Nell appears around the corner. She looks furious.

"I'd better go," I say to Lexie, and put my phone back in my jeans pocket.

Nell stands in front of me, blocking my escape.

"I was just looking for . . ."

"This?" Nell holds up my damp-with-dog-slobber school tie.

"Thanks." I take it with my fingertips. "Where did you find it?"

"*Not* behind a locked door."

Which straightaway makes me wonder what I would find there.

Darkling Cottage
Wednesday, 13 November, 1918

To dear Alfred,

You'll be glad to know I woke feeling better today, though Mama insists I stay in bed. I've never known a day pass so slowly. I've stared at my wallpaper so much I'm now seeing yellow roses when I shut my eyes. Even worse is that Mama keeps the fire burning and refuses to open any windows. Yet despite all this, I have an EXCITING thing to share.

Poor Maisie was taken home to her parents last night. (This is not the exciting part.) It's feared she has the 'flu much worse than me and is in a sorry state indeed. Maisie's so fond of you, Alfred. On hearing the war was over, she saved the top of the milk just for you in case you arrived in time for supper. I so hope she's back with us when you arrive home.

Mama only told me all this after a complete stranger brought me breakfast. I'm afraid I screamed—well, the silly girl made me jump out of my skin! The noise brought Mama running. And so I was introduced to Anna, our temporary housemaid.

Afterward, I sat in a chair while Anna washed my hair, which was still damp from last night's fever. She wasn't gentle like Maisie nor did she sing soppy songs. She was rather harsh with the comb and laughed at how filthy the water had turned. You see her hair's cut short at the neck—bobbed, she calls it, and says it's easy to keep tidy. She's quite the modern girl. She wears her skirts inches above her ankles too, and when she speaks she looks you in the eye. But I should be grateful: after all, she has offered to post this letter.

Sorry to run on. That isn't the exciting part either.

It being a sunny day, I asked Anna to open the windows. I knew Mama wouldn't approve. The fresh air made me cough rather and I was still weak, but it was good just to see the outside world. Blue sky, dead leaves, shining wet grass—everything looked super-bright.

NOW comes the EXCITING part!

Sitting at the window, I saw something move between the trees. It looked like a handkerchief or a slip blown free of the washing line. Yet even between gusts it kept moving, and I knew then it couldn't be laundry. And before you ask, I was most definitely awake.

As it came closer to the window, my heart began to race. This thing I gazed at was just like the people I saw yesterday on the path. Its tiny form was dressed in green and on its back were the most incredible little fast-beating wings.

Oh, Alfred, it was such a sight!

Even more wonderful was that in watching it, I felt suddenly completely revived. My legs lost their ache and my head cleared. I even felt a little less sad for Maisie.

It got me thinking, Alfred. Papa may have been teasing when he called me a Chime Child, yet I wonder if there's some truth in it. What I saw out the window now was definitely something magical. But other than you, I didn't know who to share it with.

When Mama came in she didn't utter a word about the open windows; she had no need to. For the windows, dear brother, were now SHUT.

Neither Anna nor I had closed them. She'd been tidying my bed, and as I've explained, I was sitting in my chair. Yet the sashes were down, the catches closed. There was no breeze. *The air in the room felt warm and still. Make of that what you will!*

I've only been ill for a day and a night, Alfred. Yet it feels different around here somehow, as if after this awful war life is finally starting to recover. I don't know quite what I mean. But there's one thing that would make things even better, and that's you being home again.

Your loving sister

11

Thursday, 14 November

The lesson before lunch is history again. By the time I reach
the classroom, Ella's already there and I see she's put her bag
on my seat.

"It's taken," she says, not looking at me.

My hand's still on the chair but I don't dare sit down. Other
people are staring now. I hear someone whisper my name.
Then Max comes in, hair on end, and flops down into his seat.

"You don't have to stand on my account, Alice," he
says. Then he sees Ella's bag. "Like that, is it?"

"She's sitting somewhere else," Ella mutters.

But there isn't anywhere to sit. Everyone's in their seats
now. Mrs. Copeland's got her back to us as she wipes the board
clean. Any second the lesson will start.

Max leans toward Ella, then swipes her bag from the chair.

"Hey!" she squeals, grabbing at it. Mrs. Copeland spins
around.

"Sit!" Max hisses to me.

I slide into my seat, very aware of Ella bristling beside me.

As soon as the lesson starts, though, it's easier to block her out. Mrs. Copeland turns the lights down and shows us black-and-white newsreel of soldiers coming home from the First World War. They're walking through a city that might be London. I'm struck by how young they look: some can't be much older than us. People watch on the pavements, in windows, on balconies, waving hankies or hats in the air. It's a cold winter's day, judging by how wrapped up everyone is and how when they speak steam puffs from their mouths. Also the trees are bare; it's funny but I'm starting to notice things like that.

Afterward, Mrs. Copeland asks us about difficult things we've faced: an argument, a disappointment, or something we've lost.

"When you're going through a bad time, what helps get you by?" She scans the room for someone to ask. I keep my eyes down so she can't pick me.

"Eating chocolate!" someone says.

We all laugh. Mrs. Copeland nods enthusiastically.

"Why do people eat chocolate?"

"Because it tastes nice?" says the same student.

"It takes your mind off the bad stuff," adds Ella.

"Good," says Mrs. Copeland. "How else might you cope with a difficult time in your life?"

Max's hand goes up. "You focus on it ending and life going back to normal again."

"*Exactly!* Excellent, Max! Think of those soldiers writing home during the war. It kept their spirits up, kept them hoping they'd go back home and get on with the lives they'd left behind. But sadly, for many, it wasn't like that. In the time they'd been away fighting, life had changed."

She tells us to put today's date in our books and the title "November 1918: How Life at Home Had Changed." We have to list all the changes we can think of: I come up with women doing men's jobs, like in factories and stuff, because the men were away fighting. Ella's page is already filling up with a mind map. When she sees me looking, she hides it with her hand. She keeps it up all during the lesson. She'll talk to Max, but if I speak, she pretends she hasn't heard me.

By the time the lunch bell rings, I've gone from upset to angry. Already today I've been told off for forgetting to do last night's homework. I've never been late with any homework before. I actually *like* the routine of it, the fact that it's boring and normal. And now I've not done my maths or French, I feel almost shaky. What I don't need is grief from Ella as well.

It's not *my* idea to cut down Darkling Wood. Left to me I'd keep the trees and try to find another way to protect the house. But what Nell's doing isn't a crime; she's just trying to stop tree roots destroying her house.

As we leave the lesson, Ella nudges Max.

"See you in the canteen?" She's clearly forgiven him for the bag incident. "I'm just going to the IT room to print something."

"Sure. Alice and I'll go ahead and get a table."

Ella pulls a "yuk" face. I'm thinking the same. I want to eat lunch without someone scowling at me over their chips.

"See you later. I'm fine on my own," I say, shouldering past them both.

Once I've got my food, I find an empty table by the window. No one else takes the other free seats; I must have "new person" disease. Either that or every student here is what Nell calls an eco-warrior, though most are dropping litter on the floor. When I check my phone for messages, there's nothing new from home. The battery's low anyway, so I stuff it back in my bag and try not to think about Lexie or Theo, who I'd give a million pounds just to see.

Looking up, I notice Max weaving his way between the tables. People wave at him, offer him a seat, but he's heading straight for me.

He drops into the chair opposite and stares at my half-eaten lunch. "So they really do sell healthy food here."

"I think it's pretending to be a salad."

Max grins. His eyes go all twinkly brown, which makes me feel a bit better. It occurs to me then that he might know Flo—he certainly knows most people around here.

"Does a girl called Flo go to this school?" I ask. "She's probably in our year group. Light brown hair, quite skinny, wears weird clothes?"

Max pulls a thinking face.

"She could be a Traveler," I add.

"Ella might know her, I suppose." I go quiet.

Max grins. "What happened to your tie?"

I untuck the crumpled end of it from my jumper. It looks a right state. "The dog chewed it."

"Ah, that old excuse," says Max. "Teachers never believe it, even when it's true."

"But it *is* true! I swear on my . . ." I stop myself mentioning Theo, though he's the first person that comes into my head. Instead, I pick up my fork and jab at a tomato.

"Sir told us about your brother," says Max. He's not grinning anymore.

"Us?"

"Ella and me."

I squish the tomato flat on the plate.

"Ella's okay, really," he says. "She's just very into conservation stuff. It makes her a bit . . . well . . . single-minded."

"But I don't want the woods cut down either. That's what's so stupid—it's pointless taking it out on me."

"It's just her way. Don't take it personally."

I look at Max. He's defending his friend and I like him for it, though I'm still wary of Ella.

Out in the corridor, the end-of-lunch bell rings. We get to our feet.

"English next," says Max. "You can sit with me if you want."

"Thanks."

I've not had a boy as a friend since preschool. I can't wait to tell Lexie later—she's bound to want all the details.

As we go out into the corridor, I stick close to Max because I don't know the way to English. There's not much room to move. A crowd of people are staring at a noticeboard on the wall. We manage to squeeze past, but then Max stops dead. I almost walk straight into the back of him.

"Oh no," he says. "She hasn't."

"What?"

"It's my fault. I'm an idiot. I overheard your grandmother's message to my dad on our answering machine. I told her what your grandmother was up to and I shouldn't have."

"Don't be daft—Ella already knew," I say, yet something in his voice makes my stomach twist.

"What's everyone looking at?"

Max doesn't answer. He grabs my sleeve and tries to rush me up the nearest stairs. But not before I see the posters. There are tons of them, A4-sized on bright green paper, stuck all over the noticeboard on top of the football team lists or whatever was there before. In big purple letters are the words:

SAVE DARKLING WOOD!

And something else underneath about a meeting. My hand covers my mouth. This must be Ella's work. I don't know if I'm going to laugh or cry. But despite what Max said, I *do* take it personally.

12

That night I go to bed early, but it's impossible to sleep. Theo, the woods, Ella's posters, all go around and around my head, and I can't make it stop.

On the floor below, the toilet flushes, then a door clicks shut. I listen as Nell settles down for the night. Soon enough, the house falls quiet but I'm more wide awake than ever, so I get up and go to the window.

That's when I see Flo. She's in the garden, directly below my window, staring up. I feel a shiver of excitement. By the time I reach the garden she's vanished, but I've an idea where I'll find her.

Sure enough, Flo's at the same spot where we last met. She's sitting cross-legged, her back against the tree trunk. I crouch down beside her. The ground's too wet for sitting, but she doesn't seem to have noticed.

"You couldn't sleep either?" I ask.

"No," she says. "And I won't until the fairies are safe again and Darkling Wood has been saved."

This feels like a dig at me for not taking her seriously.

"I'm sorry I don't believe in your fairy stuff," I say. One look at her face and it's clear she's not about to let me off the hook.

"Then you'll have to keep trying," says Flo. "Because bad things will happen if your grandmother destroys this wood."

"What bad things?"

She sighs. "I've explained this already, Alice. The fairies will take revenge. Weren't you listening?"

"I was, but . . . *seriously?*" I say. "Nell's set on cutting down the trees. I don't think she'll change her mind if I tell her there are fairies in the wood."

"She doesn't have to. You're the one the fairies have chosen. They want *you* to believe in them. I mean it, Alice. If you don't, then their magic might not be strong enough to save the wood."

It sounds nuts. But for some reason I feel a twinge in my stomach. I get to my feet.

"You can't just *make* someone believe in something that doesn't exist," I say. "It's ridiculous!"

"Fairies *do* exist, that's my point," says Flo. "They aren't just tiny creatures from storybooks. They make trouble for people who interfere in their world."

"How do you know?" I ask.

Flo hesitates. "Once, a long time ago, I did something that angered the fairies."

I look at her.

"Like what?"

"Never mind that now," she says, fiddling with her coat cuffs because she can't meet my eye. "But I know how awful their revenge can be."

Sat there under the tree she looks so pale, so lost, I almost believe her. But I still can't make sense of what she's saying.

"So let me get this straight," I say. "The fairies are already working against my grandmother."

"Yes. They rubbed the crosses off the trees, and they're the reason no tree surgeon is willing to do the job."

"But a man came yesterday. You saw him."

Flo sighs impatiently. "Yes, and there will be *more* delays, *more* mischief, just you wait and see. The fairies will use all the magic they can to try to change Nell's mind. But it might not be enough. If it isn't and the trees come down, then they'll be out for revenge."

I think of Theo. My stomach twinges, harder this time. Flo sees she's got my full attention now.

"The fairies should be able to stop your grandmother before it's too late. But that'll depend on you, Alice."

I wish she'd stop saying that.

"I just don't see why it has to be me," I say.

Flo shrugs. She doesn't seem to know either. "You need to believe in fairies, Alice. If you do then their magic is more likely to succeed. If you don't, then . . . well, I don't know what we'll do."

Flo sees how confused I am. Getting to her feet, she points to a place about six feet up the tree.

"That is a fairy door."

Now I laugh. Just once. Then cough to cover it up when I see Flo looking cross.

"Sorry," I say. "Honestly, how do you know all this stuff?"

"A fairy expert once told me."

"A *fairy expert*?"

Flo frowns at me. "Will you please listen?"

"Sorry," I say again.

She takes a deep breath. "Look at where the trunk splits in two. It forms a gap, a space. See it?"

I nod.

"Good. Now, do you see how, just a few feet higher up, the trunk comes back together again?"

"Yes." Where the trunk splits it forms an oblong hole in the tree. It's possible to see right through to the other side.

"That space is a fairy door," says Flo.

"A *fairy door*?"

She gives me a pained look. "Oh, do stop repeating everything I say."

"Sorry," I say, yet again. It's probably easier just to play along. "So, how does it work?"

"A fairy door is a very magical place. It's a boundary between our world and theirs." She beckons me over.

"Come and have a look."

The bottom of the fairy door is above the top of my head. I have to stand on my highest tiptoes and pull myself up with my hands to look through it.

"What do you see?" Flo asks.

"Um . . . trees . . . dead leaves . . . the woods. Why, what am I looking for?"

"Fairies, obviously." She's getting grumpy again. "Think of it as a window rather than a door. Look through it, concentrate a little, and you might see fairies."

"*I am* looking, but I can't see anything."

Flo sighs. "All right. You can stop now. It's probably too soon."

I'm about to ask what she means when my left hand, still gripping the branch, finds a dip in the wood.

Something's stuffed inside it. As I touch it, it crackles. What I take out is a piece of paper.

"Is it yours?" I ask, turning to Flo. She shakes her head.

The paper is folded over. It's thick. Good quality. As I open it, I see five words. The letters are black. Capitals. Written so big they fill the page.

PLEASE KEEP MY BROTHER SAFE.

I fold it back up again so I don't have to look at it.

"Did you write this?" I ask. "How do you even *know* about Theo?"

"But I didn't write it, I promise," says Flo. "Perhaps it was the fairies. Their magic is especially strong in this tree—it's a beech tree, you see, and beeches have special properties."

"How's that got *anything* to do with my brother?" I say. My voice shakes with anger.

Flo tries to take my hand, but I snatch it away. I don't want any of this to be about Theo. I don't even want to talk about him right now. It scares me. I screw up the piece of paper and stuff it back in the tree.

"I'm sorry, Flo, but this is stupid. I don't believe any of this. I . . . just . . . can't."

Flo nods. Takes a step away from me. She's crying now, which makes me feel bad.

"I'm sorry too," she says. "I don't think you quite realize how awful this could become. If your grandmother cuts down this wood, then the fairies will . . ."

"I can't listen to this, Flo," I say, shaking my head. "My brother is being cared for by doctors in a top London hospital. *Fairies* have got nothing to do with it."

"Not yet," she says.

I stare at her. I can't think how to reply.

"Goodbye, Flo," I say. I've had enough.

Nell's waiting for me in the kitchen.

"Well?" she says.

"Well, what?"

"Don't take that tone with me," she says.

I wonder if she's about to slap me. She doesn't; she locks the back door and puts the key in her pajama pocket.

"Let's start again, shall we?" she says. I fold my arms.

"Borage woke me," she says. "He was whining at my bedroom door because *someone* had been downstairs and let him out of the kitchen."

"Oh." I feel my face go red. "I didn't mean to."

"Your shoes were gone too," she says. "And your coat. Where have you been, Alice?"

"Why?"

"I won't have this!" she says.

"Won't have what?" I know I'm being lippy, but I'm angry too.

"This wandering about like you own the place. First I catch you poking about upstairs, now you're going off in the middle of the night. It's got to stop!"

"I was only in the woods."

"Doing what exactly?"

I look at my feet. "Nothing."

"Nothing?"

"All right, I couldn't sleep, so I went and had a look at that tree."

"Which tree?"

"The one . . ." I hesitate because this is going to sound nuts. ". . . with the fairy door . . ."

Nell leans on the table like she's dizzy. "Who told you about that tree?"

I don't answer.

But I've landed myself in it now because Flo's not allowed in the wood and it was my job to tell her. Nell doesn't wait for me to speak. She starts shouting inches from my face.

"Did you climb it?"

"Of course not! Why *would* I?"

"Because if I think for one second you've been climbing trees, you'll stay in your room for the next *month*, do you hear me?"

"I won't be here that long," I mutter.

She's breathing fast. She won't look at me.

"Bed!" she says, pointing to the door. "And that's an order."

Up in my room, I try to phone Mum. If by some miracle I get a signal, I'll beg her to take me home. But my phone's completely dead and when I search my stuff, I realize I've lost the charger. I climb into bed and cry myself empty. No one here can make it better—not Flo, not Nell, not the trees. The people I love most are two hours away by car, but it might as well be another country. Stuck here I can't do anything except wait. And hope. Though it seems I'm not much good at either.

Darkling Cottage
Thursday, 14 November, 1918

Dear Alfred,

    I've come to bed early, for I've lots to tell you, though I have hardly enough ink to write it all down.

    You'll remember Mama's been wanting Papa to take up a hobby. Well, he's chosen photography. I don't know about you, Alfred, but I've only ever seen a camera at school when Mrs. Burgess made us line up by the front wall and smile for a man who ducked his head under a blanket to take the picture.

Papa's camera is much smaller. It's called a "Midg" and is a black boxy shape about the size of a satchel. There's a lens at the front, and the back opens like a door. It's a surprisingly simple-looking gadget.

Anyhow, today—after much pleading—I was allowed downstairs to sit in the library with Papa. I'd hoped we might talk some more about this Chime Child business, but alas he was busy developing pictures. Strange bottles and trays of liquid covered every available surface. It was as if our library was now a laboratory, and our Papa a mad scientist! I think the title "Dr. Waterhouse" would rather suit him, don't you?

Truly, Alfred, it was fascinating to watch him at work. Slowly, but surely, little shadowy shapes appeared on the paper, and then Papa pegged each piece onto a sort of clothesline to dry.

We waited. And waited some more. Then Papa checked his pictures and got cross (his temper is very short these days) because they'd not developed properly after all.

Well, I didn't care to stay after that. But the fire in the drawing room hadn't yet been laid, and I couldn't bear to go back upstairs. Pulling on my coat, I went to the woods. And there, under our special beech tree, I soon forgot Papa's short temper and his stupid pictures.

Last time you were home, we lay at this very spot and stared up at the sun until our eyes went funny, didn't we? Well, there was no sun today. If you'd been here we'd have climbed up to the special O-shaped place where the trunk splits in two. But you weren't here, Alfred, and without you everything feels so difficult.

So I made do with climbing to the lowest branch, and gazed out over Glossop's meadow. At some point, I happened to look down.

At the foot of the tree, the grass was moving. I suspected a rabbit, maybe a fox, but no animal emerged and yet the grass kept twitching. How odd it sounds! Well, prepare yourself. It gets odder still. Even writing of it makes my heart skip a beat.

As suddenly as it started, the grass went very still.

Then, before my eyes, little figures began to emerge from the undergrowth—I counted ten in total. None was taller than a foot in height. Just like the ones I'd seen before, they looked as human as you or I, only much, much smaller. Some had pale skin, some had dark, yet they all wore the same garment—a pale green tunic made of thin, gauzy stuff, which caught the light as they moved.

And move they did, rushing from one tree to the next. It was like watching ants at work, or bees in a hive. And how their tiny wings fluttered, just like a butterfly's!

They knew I was watching them. A few dipped their heads at me in a kind of greeting. Another flew up to hover at my feet, inspecting me just as I'd inspected them. All the time I barely moved. Indeed, I held my breath for such long intervals my lungs felt ready to burst!

Eventually, the sky grew dark and I knew it must be near teatime. The little people faded from sight until all that remained was ten perfect circles of flattened grass.

When I slid down from the tree, I'd grown stiff and very

cold. *And yet in all other respects, I felt very well. For the first time in ages, it seemed as if nothing was missing—not even you, Alfred. I felt COMPLETE.*

Back home, I spoke to Mrs. Cotter of what I'd seen. You'll remember how she is with old sayings and superstitions, so I didn't suppose she'd think me queer. She said she'd never seen any creatures in the wood, unless I meant squirrels and rabbits, and she'd seen plenty of both.

Yet there are such things as fairies, Alfred. And despite what people think, it appears they live in our wood.

Your very excited sister

13

Friday, 15 November

At breakfast we don't speak, which makes things easier. There's a plan in my head that's growing so fast I can't concentrate on anything. I'm spilling milk, dropping sugar, fumbling about in the cutlery drawer. It's like I've got sausages for fingers. As Nell makes coffee, I slip Borage my toast because I can't eat a thing.

Eventually I break the silence.

"Can I have some lunch money, please?"

"You must have a hole in your pocket, young lady. Didn't I give you five pounds yesterday?"

She did. It's still in my purse. The lie makes my face burn. But she's too busy picking papers up off the table to notice.

"Over there," Nell says, waving vaguely at the dresser. "In the cake tin."

Once she's left the room, I get the cake tin down. Inside is a wad of notes—easily enough to get to London—but taking it feels wrong. So I tell myself I'm doing this for Theo. I've had enough of fairies and trees and bad magic. I just want to make sure my little brother is all right. Dad might not want to visit him, but I really do. And I promise myself I'll pay Nell back when I can.

The school bus is packed as usual. I make a beeline for the back seats, where the older people who go to college sit, because today I'm going to ride with them all the way into town. Some of the Ferndean kids turn around in their seats like they can't believe what I'm doing. There's one free place at the back, though someone's bag is on it. As the bus lurches forward, I trip down the aisle. The older kids laugh. Right now, I'd happily die of embarrassment.

"Oh, let her sit down, Dan!" someone says.

There's much eye rolling, but the boy's clearly kinder than Ella, because he does move his bag.

"Thanks," I say.

I shrink into the seat, hugging my bag with Theo's card safe inside it. The older kids soon forget I'm here. They're talking about a TV show I've never heard of. Once I've checked my purse is still in my pocket, I try to breathe normally again.

Sixteen minutes later, we reach Ferndean High. The bus swings into the driveway and stops. The kids down the front get off. I shrink further into my seat. The older kids keep talking. I can't believe I'm about to skip school. I'd never do something this daring at home.

Then, just as the bus doors shut, the boy next to me turns around.

"Hey," he says, looking at my blazer. "Shouldn't you be . . . ?"

More faces peer around my seat. I hug my bag even tighter to my chest. They're going to tell. I know they are. I bite my lip.

"Reckon we've got a skiver here," a girl with a silver nose stud says, and suddenly they're all patting me on the shoulder like I've just scored a goal.

"Respect," says the boy next to me. He raises his hand so we do a clumsy high five. It makes me feel stupidly chuffed.

"Your secret's safe with us," says the nose-stud girl, and offers me some gum.

I take it. The bus moves on. So far, so good.

We join a main road. The traffic's heavy so we slow right down. It seems to take forever. Finally we stop alongside a gray building, where hundreds of students are hanging around outside on the pavement.

"Westway College, ladies and gents," says the driver. The older kids groan and stand up super-slowly. All I've got to do now is sneak past the driver. Once I'm off, I'll find the station. It should be easy.

But no one's shifting. They're all bickering about who's left crisp packets on the floor. The driver joins in; it's a different one today. She gets up from her seat and comes down the aisle. One minute she's talking litter, the next her eyes fall on me. I'm the only one here in school uniform.

"Hang on," she says. "You were meant to get off at Ferndean."

It goes silent. Everyone's looking at me. My heart starts to race.

"Not today," I say, which isn't exactly a lie.

"Got a note, have you?"

I haven't. Not even a pretend one.

"Excuse me." I push past her before she can blink. The big kids cheer me on. It feels good. I can do this.

Out on the pavement, I'm surrounded by students hugging folders to their chests. The bus driver shouts something, but no one takes any notice. There's safety in numbers, I think, and stay hovering in the crowd until the bus finally pulls away from the curb. Only then do I start walking. I've not the foggi-est where the station is, but there's a shop selling newspapers on the corner of the street. So I go in to ask.

The woman behind the counter thinks I'm bunking, I can tell. But she points out where the station is and mentions a shortcut through the park. I'm nervous again now. Gut-churning, sweaty-hands nervous. But as I go through the park, I find I'm noticing the trees. *Oak, ash, beech.* A few days ago I didn't know one tree from another.

The park ends at a pair of tall green gates. Up ahead I see traffic lights. More cars, buses, trucks. And there's a road sign with a symbol on it, that red one with white lines. My stomach does a flip. It means I'm nearly there.

Minutes later, I'm at the station. The glass doors close behind me and I walk along a passage that runs underground. It's echoey and smells like old toilets. There are people every-where, carrying bags, dragging those wheelie suitcases, drink-ing takeaway coffee. I check that my purse is still in my coat pocket and head for the platform.

There's a bing-bong on the PA, then a voice:

"The next train to arrive at platform four is the nine-twenty-five to . . ."

I don't hear the rest. There's a great whooshing sound, a screech of brakes, and the stink of hot rubber. People swarm around me. I'm jammed up against someone's bag, someone's pushchair. I look for the ticket machine but I can't see a thing. The crowd shuffles forward, taking me with it. I try to turn around but can't move.

Then somehow I'm inside the train. There are people still piling on behind me. Out on the platform, a whistle blows. The doors hiss shut. I'm going somewhere, but I've no idea where.

14

The train gets up speed. I don't have a ticket. I don't know where I'm heading. And I'm sure it's obvious as I loiter near the luggage rack, sweating. I'd stick out less if I sat down in a seat. So I find somewhere quiet in a nearby carriage. There's an old lady doing a crossword sitting across the aisle. She looks like a safe person to speak to.

"Excuse me," I say. "Is this the train for London?"

She nods. "Just one stop at Reading."

I shut my eyes in relief.

We go through a tunnel that makes my ears pop, then over miles and miles of flat, flooded fields. Theo would love to be here right now. This window seat is perfect for playing "count the crows."

First one to spot a hundred crows is the winner.

We've played it on so many journeys. It's a Campbell family tradition. The winner gets the best flavor crisps from the multipack for lunch, which we all know are cheese and onion.

I don't hear the carriage door open. When I look around there's a man in a dark blue suit asking to see tickets. If I'm nice and polite he'll let me buy one now, won't he? I didn't mean to get caught in the crowds. Reaching into my coat pocket, my hand freezes. An awful sinking feeling hits me.

Oh no. Please. No.

I check the other pocket. My purse was here! I double-check again. Check the other pocket. Check my bag.

The ticket man reaches me.

"I need to buy a ticket." By now I'm hot to the tips of my ears. "But I can't find my purse."

"Is that so?" says the ticket man, like he's heard the excuse hundreds of times.

I pat my pockets frantically as if it'll make my purse reappear. The ticket man stares down at me. I take a gulp of air. This is all going wrong.

"Look, I'm not a criminal," I say. "I'm just going to see my brother."

"Not without a ticket, you're not."

He says I have to get off at the next stop. There's a fine to pay too. And he wants my name and address, though it's got to go on a special form.

"They're at the front of the train," the man says. "You'd better come with me."

I get up. People are looking at me now, which makes me go even redder. We walk down the aisle, through the sliding doors and into the next carriage. A few passengers glance up as we pass but I keep my eyes firmly on the ticket man's back.

Then, as we go into another carriage, someone puts out a hand. The ticket man stops.

"Yes, sir?"

"Could you tell me which train . . ."

I don't hear the rest. Just behind me on the other side of the doors is the toilet. There's a sign on it saying "Out of order." It's my chance. I need to be brave. Tell myself I can do this, that getting to London is easier—*far easier*—than starting at a new school.

Any moment, the ticket inspector will stop talking and start walking again. It's now or never. I take a step back. Then another. I'm through the sliding doors. The ticket man hasn't even turned around.

Inside, the toilet stinks. There's wet tissue all over the floor and the sink's blocked. I lock the door quick. Within seconds, someone's banging on it. I go very still. The handle wiggles.

"You in there?" says the ticket man.

I hold my breath.

It goes quiet. He must've gone. Lid down, I crouch on top of the loo seat. And wait. Near Reading the train starts to slow. It stops, the carriage doors open, and there's thumping and rustling as luggage is put in the racks. Someone tries the door again. Then I hear the ticket man's voice.

"Well, she's not in there now. She must've got off here and given us the slip."

I just hope this means he'll leave me alone. The train judders. And then we're away again. Next stop London.

Not long to go. I try not to think of Nell. School will have phoned by now to say I'm absent and she'll be fuming. And I bet she's called Mum, who'll be all stressed out. I get a stab of guilt. Mum doesn't need anything extra to worry about. Perhaps this wasn't such a brilliant idea.

Too late now. The train makes that *clackety-clack* sound as we begin to slow down. Standing on the wet floor, I get ready to run.

The PA comes on.

"We are now approaching Paddington. . . ."

I shift my bag onto my shoulder. The train squeals to a halt. I ease the toilet door open.

Out on the platform, everyone's walking toward a barrier. A ticket barrier. I hesitate. Someone bumps into me.

"Watch it, love," the person says.

At the barrier, the crowd thins into three lines. I join the longest because I need time to work out what to do. There must be a way to get through without a ticket. The queue shuffles forward.

I'm just four people away from the barrier now. The floor's swept clean—no sign of any dropped tickets.

Three people away. Two . . .

"Got you!"

I'm jerked backward. I try to turn around, but the ticket man's gripping my bag. He's almost pulled me off my feet. Instinctively I lunge forward. Something rips. The ticket man still holds on to me. And then, quite suddenly, he lets go.

I don't think: I run, scrambling over the ticket barrier like it's life or death. Once I'm clear of the station, I slow down. The remains of my bag strap hangs off my left shoulder. There's no bag attached; I suppose the ticket man's still holding on to it.

If Lexie were here, we'd die laughing. But I'm on my own with no money, no phone, and no idea how to reach the hospital. It's not even remotely funny. Nor's the fact that Theo's card is still inside my bag. I've come all this way to give it to him, and now I can't even do that.

To make things worse, it's started to rain. A red bus goes by, then a taxi, then more taxis. Some have their lights on, which means they're for hire—not that it's any good to me. Stuffing my hands in my pockets, I walk faster. I don't know if

I'm going in the right direction but it makes me feel like I'm not giving up. After all, I've made it this far. I'm here in London. Theo can't be far away.

At the end of the road, there's one of those big maps of the area done for tourists. I'm so glad I want to throw my arms right around it; a bit of luck at last! Finding the "You Are Here" dot, I then work out where the hospital is. It looks like a long walk down a straight main road.

A few turnings and I'm on that road. It's noisy and smelly. Greasy-looking pigeons swoop around the traffic. Everywhere is gray: gray tarmac, gray buildings, gray sky. It looks strange after Darkling Wood, where everything is green or brown or blue.

At another of the tourist maps, I check my bearings. I'm still on track. The rain's turned into that sharp, sleety stuff that stings your skin. But it doesn't matter because it's not far to go now and I can't wait to see Mum and Theo's faces when they see me. I get a fizz of excitement in my tummy. Or it might be nerves. Head down against the rain, I walk faster. The next turning should be it.

15

Last time I was here it was dark. Even now, in daylight, the building is achingly familiar with its glass-roofed entrance and the blue NHS sign on the wall.

I breathe deeply. I've made it.

In through the sliding doors, I'm hit by that hospital smell of cabbage and antiseptic. Everywhere I look there's doctors, wheelchairs, trolleys, teddy bear–shaped balloons on sticks. There's a queue at reception, so I find the elevators and jump in just as the doors are closing.

"Which floor, love?" says a lady doing the buttons.

"Cheetah Ward" is all I can remember.

"Fourth floor," she says.

We start to go up. I'm fidgety as anything. There are other people in the elevator. No one speaks. Everyone's watching the buttons light up.

First floor . . . second floor . . . Each one takes me nearer to Theo.

At the fourth floor, the doors open. I'm the only person getting out. Cheetah Ward is just down the corridor. There's a mural on the wall, showing wild animals and flowers. It looks as nice as a hospital can look.

The doors to the ward are locked so I press a bell. No one comes. I press again. My legs start jiggling. Finally a nurse comes out. She's dressed in blue with a face mask around her neck. Her name badge tells me she's called Jo.

"Can I help you?" Jo says.

I tuck my hair behind my ears. Stand up tall. "I'm here to see Theo Campbell, please."

"And you are?"

"His sister, Alice."

"Aha, I've heard about you." Jo smiles. "Your mum tells me you've been a real star these past months."

Though my cheeks go hot, I smile back.

"Is your gran with you?" she says, glancing over my shoulder.

"No, she doesn't like hospitals."

"Me neither," says Jo. She's joking, I think. She doesn't seem in any hurry to let me in, either.

"So can I see him?" I ask.

"Sorry, but the rules are only two visitors per bedside," Jo says. "And now you're here, that makes three."

I don't quite follow. Mum's here and . . . *who else?*

Jo answers for me. "I'll tell your parents you're here."

Parents.

I'm not smiling now.

That means Mum and . . . *Dad?*

So he did come after all.

Jo's seen the shock on my face; she gives my arm a quick squeeze. "I'll see what I can do."

At the door, she stops to use the hand gel, then she's gone again.

I lean against the wall. My head's reeling. Of all the things I'd expected today, Dad wasn't on the list.

Don't expect me to be pleased, I think. I came all this way to visit Theo, not Dad, who hasn't seen us for months. Who didn't even think it was important enough to come straight to the hospital when Theo was admitted. So if there's too many visitors *he* can leave, not me.

The door to the ward flies open. Mum rushes out into the corridor.

"Alice, sweetheart!" she cries, throwing her arms around me. "What are you doing here? Where's Nell?"

I hug her back. She smells different. Not of soap powder like she usually does, but as if she's been in these clothes for days. She clings on so tight it's hard to breathe.

"You're suffocating me," I say.

Mum lets go. There's a pause. She looks tired. Her hair's all dirty and there are shadows under her eyes. She's not smiling either.

"I promised Theo I'd come," I say. "I've missed him so much. I couldn't wait any longer."

"I'm sorry, darling. It's been . . ." Mum's face crumples and she starts to cry. Then I remember Dad's here somewhere too and I bet that's why she's upset. There are some fold-down seats on the wall opposite. Going over to them, we sit. Mum cries a bit more, then blows her nose and takes a shuddery breath.

"Is Nell waiting outside?" she asks.

I know then that Nell hasn't phoned Mum. That Mum doesn't know I've come here by myself. So I tell her.

She gasps. "You didn't! Oh, Alice!"

"Shush, Mum," I say. "I'm here now, so stop fussing."

"But what about school? And Nell? Oh, Alice, tell me she knows you're here!"

I fiddle with my coat sleeves.

Mum peers into my face. "She doesn't know, does she?"

"No."

Mum groans. I hoped she'd be pleased to see me but this isn't going according to plan.

"I'd better call her now," she says, getting out her phone. She stands up and walks a little way down the corridor. There's the murmur of voices, but I can't hear exactly what's being said.

"School called her earlier to say you'd not turned up. She's not happy with you, you know," Mum says as she sits down again. "But you'll have to deal with that when you get back."

I don't want to think about Nell. Or school. Or going back. I'm here to see my brother and that's all that matters.

"How is Theo?" I ask.

She shrugs. I wait for the cheery comment, the big smile, the little joke, but instead her eyes go teary again and my insides fall away. Things *aren't* right, are they? I wasn't just imagining it over the phone.

"Can I see him?" I ask, getting to my feet. "Will you come with me?"

What I mean is, I don't want to be in there with Dad. I want it just to be Theo, Mum, and me.

"It's only two visitors per bed," Mum sniffs. "Your dad's with him now."

"So tell Dad to go."

Mum blinks slowly. She looks done in.

The ward door swings open. It's Jo, the nurse. Behind her is my dad. "Looks like he's leaving anyway," says Mum.

Except Dad's not leaving. Brushing past Jo, he walks

straight up to us. As I get ready to be cross with him, Mum jumps to her feet.

"What is it, David?" she says. "What's happened?" Then Dad sees me.

"Wow … I m-mean … Alice," he stutters. "This is a … surprise."

He looks terrible. Worse than Mum. His eyes are all pouchy underneath and his stubble's got gray bits in it. He looks *old*.

"Is Nell with you?" he asks, glancing up and down the corridor.

Because I don't answer, Mum chips in. "She came by herself."

"Oh. Right." Unlike Mum, he seems almost relieved.

Jo joins us.

"You'd better come in," she says.

"What's going on?" Mum sounds scared; I don't like it.

"Please, just come back inside. The doctor wants to have a chat with you."

She directs Mum and Dad back through the door. No one mentions visitor numbers now, so as we pause to wash our hands in antiseptic gel, I slip in too. The door clicks shut behind us.

We set off down a corridor that's got strip lights all along the ceiling. It makes my eyes hurt. Then we go through another set of doors, past children wired up to drips and machines that beep.

We're walking quickly. There's another beep. This one's nearer. It's Jo's pager. Instantly she's running. So are Mum and Dad. I don't know what's happening, but now I'm running too.

16

We race down a bright white corridor. Up ahead are more nurses. Lots more nurses. They're gathered in the doorway to a room. On the wall, above the door, a single red light flashes. When we reach them, the nurses make way for Jo.

"What's happening?" Mum stands on tiptoes. "Let me through!"

This must be Theo's room. I should be glad: I'm here at last.

But it's wrong. All wrong.

The room's crowded. I can't even see the bed. They won't let Mum in so I don't stand a chance. Other people in different uniforms come in and out. They're talking in big words I don't understand.

Mum starts sobbing again. Dad tries to put an arm around her.

"Don't you dare!" she spits, pulling away from him. She lets me hold her hand.

We stay out in the corridor, not speaking. Just waiting. Dad paces up and down, doing big heavy sighs. Time slows to a crawl. But at some point the alarm goes quiet and the lights stop flashing. A doctor comes out of the room.

"Mr. Campbell?" she says. "Mrs. Campbell?"

Mum ignores the mistake and straightens up. Dad stops pacing. I fight the urge to cry.

The doctor looks at me. "Why don't you make some tea for your parents? There's a little kitchen two doors down."

What she means is: this isn't a conversation for kids.

Mum keeps hold of my hand. "We don't want tea, thank you."

"Carrie, please," says Dad. "Be sensible. The doctor needs to speak to us and it might not be suitable"—his eyes flit over me—"for Alice to hear."

"I'm all right," I say, because I know how sick Theo is. Unlike Dad, I've actually been there for him ever since he got ill.

"She's staying," says Mum.

The doctor pushes her glasses up her nose. "Okay, so Theo's not been doing too well on his antibiotics and now he's had a reaction—quite a severe one. But we've managed to stabilize him," she says.

Mum squeezes my hand.

"But I warn you, he's still very poorly. We've changed the medication, and I'm hopeful this will reduce his temperature."

"Thank you," Mum whispers.

The doctor nods. "The first few days after a transplant are often the most difficult."

We all go quiet.

Then Dad says, "Will he make it?"

Mum gasps. "Don't ask that, David!"

I hear the doctor's hesitation. It's horrible.

"We'll have to wait and see," she says finally.

My bottom lip starts to wobble. Dad nods. Stuffs his hands in his jeans pockets and looks at Mum. His eyes are very hard.

"Will you stay with Theo?" he says. "Only Lara's called to say . . ."

"Go," says Mum, turning away. "Just . . . *go.*"

"But Alice shouldn't really be here. It's too much for her."

I can't believe he's saying this. I stare at him in amazement. "It's not *too much* for me, Dad!"

The doctor looks embarrassed. "If we could maybe just . . ."

Mum cuts in. "Your daughter's made of strong stuff, David. If you'd paid her more attention you'd know that."

Dad doesn't say anything. He rubs a hand over his face. Then he swings around and slams his fist into the wall.

I flinch. Mum looks away.

"Mr. Campbell," the doctor says. "Please . . ."

But Dad's already halfway down the corridor. He doesn't look back. The doors swing shut and he's gone. Part of me's glad. The other part is mad at him for running back to his new family because it's easier than staying here with us. I can't think about that now, though. All I want is my brother.

"You can see Theo if you like," the doctor says, then glances at me. "You haven't got a cold? No tummy bugs?"

I shake my head.

"Good. The medication he's on makes it hard for him to fight germs." She gestures toward Theo's door.

"Just sit with him. Let him know you're there."

Mum goes in first with me behind her. Jo's the only nurse left here now. She's writing something down but glances up at us.

"He had everyone worried, then," she says, trying to smile but not quite managing it. "I'll leave you alone."

As she goes, my eyes follow her. I can't bring myself to look at the bed. The room feels too hot. It smells of antiseptic and rubber. There's a little high-up window, and through a gap in the curtains I see the glass is streaked with rain. Perhaps it's raining right now in Darkling Wood; I almost hear it falling through the trees. But very soon those trees will be gone, which makes me feel more miserable.

"Alice?" says Mum. Her voice makes me jump. "Sit down and say hello to your brother."

She's pulled up a chair for me. I sink into it. Mum sits down on the other side of the bed. Theo lies between us, a shape under a white blanket. He hasn't said a word. I suppose he's fast asleep; he's not normally this quiet. Though I still can't look at his face, his hand is at eye level, so I stare at that instead.

It's a very small hand. The back of it is covered in tape to hold the needle thing in place. I think of that hand gripping a plastic dinosaur. Now it's lying limp on a blanket. Really I should take hold of it, stroke it, squeeze it just so he knows I'm here.

The thing is, I can't.

A heart that stopped five days ago now beats in my brother's chest. The stranger must've had a donor card, and something of that kind stranger lives on in this room, pumping the blood inside those veins that stand out on the back of Theo's hand. It's really strange. Almost as if he isn't quite *Theo* anymore, now part of him was once someone else.

"Your big sister's come to see you, Theo," says Mum. "Aren't you lucky?"

A machine beeps away by the bedside. Theo doesn't move.

I wipe my eyes on my sleeve. He's not lucky. A proper sister would've brought games and sweets, all wrapped up. I couldn't even manage to bring the stupid card I made. I've come all this way just to sit on a chair. Despite what the doctor said, he doesn't know I'm here.

When I do look at his face, it knocks me sideways. He's definitely not Theo. He can't be. He's as white as the bedsheets. His eyes are closed; the lids seem bruised, almost greasy. He's got tubes up his nose and in his mouth, and down the middle of his chest is a line of white tape.

It makes my own heart thud.

Looking up, I see Dad's come back; he's in the doorway.

"Is he asleep?" he asks.

Mum doesn't answer; she keeps talking to Theo in a dreamy lullaby voice. Dad gazes at the window, the floor, the ceiling. He can't seem to look at Theo either. It's funny, I think, all four of us being together in the same room. I can't remember the last time this happened. It doesn't feel good.

Mum glances at me. "You all right, Alice?"

"She's gone a funny color," says Dad.

"I'm fine," I say, though I'm not. I just don't want to prove him right. I try to breathe deeply, but panic simmers inside me. Everything looks too bright. I wonder if I'm about to be sick. I get to my feet.

"I need some fresh air."

I rush for the exit, through double doors, past nurses and doctors and worried-looking relatives until I'm out into the corridor with the animals on the wall. Dad's right behind me.

"Go away!" I say. "Leave me alone!"

But then my mouth fills up and I start to retch. His hand rubs my back until I'm done.

Darkling Cottage
Friday, 15 November, 1918

Dearest Alfred,

This is a very important letter because I'm writing it to prove you're still alive. Today we received a telegram. It said you were "Missing, believed killed." The delivery boy swore it was official but I WON'T believe it, not now we're five days into peace.

Today was fated from the start. We'd had heavy rain in the night, which made the roads so tricky that Anna was late coming in from the village. So when the front doorbell rang, there was no Anna to answer it. And as Mrs. Cotter was up to her elbows in flour, I said I'd go.

I wasn't expecting to find the telegram boy on our doorstep. I remember thinking that his ears looked cold because he'd taken off his cap. Propped up against his hip was his red Post Office bicycle—blood-red, people often said. I wondered how he'd managed to ride it down our lane, which was running with water like a river.

Even then it didn't occur to me. Why would it? The war is over. What bad news could a telegram bring us now?

Behind me, I heard footsteps. Then Mama was at my side, asking where Anna was and why on earth was I standing on a wet doorstep with not even a shawl about me. I think she would've gone on, only the sight of the telegram boy stopped her.

He held out a pen; he said he needed a signature, please. Mama frowned. Then she saw the telegram in his other hand. As she took it from him, her face fell. The War Office stamp was on the envelope and Papa's name, "Mr. Henry Waterhouse." The date mark was 20th October, 1918.

20th October, Alfred. Nearly one month ago. Before peace was declared.

Mama started shaking her head. I felt suddenly scared. There must be some mistake, she said, and tried to give the telegram back. But the boy held up his hands and said he was sorry, it was meant for us. Sometimes news got delayed, he said. Sometimes it got lost altogether and then families never knew. I can't imagine which would be worse.

Mama didn't open the telegram all day. She hid it behind the clock on the drawing-room mantelpiece, then put on her best hat and went out. I didn't like being left alone with it, especially when a little corner of the envelope was still in view. Part of me itched to read what it said. But mostly I wished I'd never ever answered that beastly doorbell.

It wasn't until after dinner that Mama finally told Papa. We'd heard so often of families in the village receiving terrible news from the Front, and here it was, happening to us. It felt like a frightful dream.

White-faced, Papa stood before the fire and opened the telegram. He shook so hard it was a wonder he didn't slice his fingers on the letter opener.

I held my breath as he read its contents out loud, then he screwed it up and threw it into the flames.

We all retired late tonight. It seemed none of us wanted to leave the fireside and go to our cold beds. It's been an awful day. We've come through the whole war, and now . . .

this . . . when you should be coming home. Instead, dearest brother, you are "missing, believed killed."

Yet the thing is, boys do come home even after they've been reported missing. Mama says it happened to Mrs. Cotter's sister's son. Apparently she heated water for his bath every night for two years, and eventually he did return.

So that's what we must do. Not the hot water part, Alfred. What I mean is we must keep hoping, and prove that rotten telegram wrong.

Your ever-loving sister

17

Saturday, 16 November

It's past midnight when Dad and I leave the hospital. The doctor wouldn't let me on the ward again just in case I have a sickness bug. But I think we all knew the real reason: seeing Theo wasn't exciting or lovely. It was like being kicked in the stomach. So all this time I've had to wait in the Relatives' Room with its pink chairs and pictures of water lilies, which I suppose are meant to be soothing. And now Dad has agreed to drive me back to Nell's and I don't have any choice in that either.

He's got a new car; it's silver and much bigger than ours. Once we've got in, he turns the heater on high and puts a carrier bag of food into my lap. I don't touch it, though my stomach's growling.

"You need to eat," Dad says. "It'll make you feel better."

"I'm fine." I don't want him to be right about something else.

Now we're by ourselves, I realize just how angry I am. It took Dad five days to get to the hospital. FIVE WHOLE DAYS. What the heck's he been doing in that time, other than ignoring Theo?

Though I'm dying to ask, I dread the excuses he'll come up with. So I stare at the wet wipes and baby snacks on the dashboard—and that's hard too. He's someone else's dad now, not just Theo's and mine.

As the car warms up, I grow tired. But when I shut my eyes I see Theo in his hospital bed, and the fear on Mum's face. It makes me feel ill again. It's better to stay awake, though once we join the motorway there's nothing much to look at anymore.

"Pass me a sandwich, would you?" says Dad.

My stomach does another growl. I've got that queasy sort of hunger. I really should eat. Inside the carrier bag there are egg sandwiches, ham and turkey, cheese and salad, and two big bags of crisps. Dad's bought orange juice and flapjacks, and a couple of red apples. Being at Nell's, I've forgotten what real food looks like.

But then, Dad can cook. *Did* cook. He'd do a roast every Sunday, make fruit pies with proper pastry and serve them with made-from-scratch custard. Just thinking about it makes my mouth water. It's shocking to think Nell's his mother. Last time we ate with him it was different, though. We had burgers in a service station somewhere and Theo was too unwell to eat. That was when he told us his girlfriend Lara was having a baby.

"Here." I pass Dad the turkey sandwich, which looks dry and boring.

He takes it and forces down a mouthful. "Today's been tough, hasn't it?"

"It's been all right," I say. I'm not about to bare my soul if that's what he's hoping. I keep eating my own sandwich.

"You knew Theo was this sick, didn't you? Mum's kept you in the picture?"

I nod.

"The whole picture, I mean. The risks, not just the positives."

I glance at him sideways.

"The thing is, Alice, your mum's pinning all her hopes on this operation, which is typical of her ..." He falters. "Don't look at me like that."

"Like what?"

"Like I'm the worst person in the world." I don't answer.

"All I'm trying to say," says Dad, "is that your mother can be quite ... *optimistic*. She doesn't always see the dangers in things."

I stare out the window. Part of me knows what he means. She's what Lexie's mum calls a "glass half full" person. But she wasn't when Dad first left, and she wasn't today, and it scares me. If Mum can't see the bright side, then maybe that's because there *is* no bright side to see.

"Alice, transplants are risky. Sometimes, people get their hopes up—they've tried all the other options and this is the last resort, and then ..." He stops.

"What?"

He rubs his eye, though I don't think he's crying. "It's a very big deal for everyone, an operation like this. I just hope it's going to make Theo better."

I scowl at my reflection in the glass. "Don't you believe in transplants, then? You think we should've just let Theo get worse?"

"Of course not! The doctors are getting better at transplants all the time, but there's always the risk that a person's body will reject the donor organ."

"They give him tablets to stop that, don't they?"

"Yes, but those tablets aren't without risk either. They make it very hard for him to fight infections."

"I know, but . . ."

"I just want you to be prepared, that's all." I wish Dad would shut up.

"Seeing Theo shocked you, didn't it?" he says. "You didn't expect him to be so sick."

My eyes start to water. That feeling I got in Theo's hospital room, of being hot and trapped, is coming back.

"I wanted to see him," I say. "I promised."

"Though I don't suppose he even knew we were there."

"How can you say that? Of course he knew I was there!"

Even so, I see flashes of Theo lying flat in his bed, his eyelids shut, his hand a bit too still.

"Oh just shut up, will you?" I slump down in my seat. We don't speak for a bit, then I turn to face Dad. He still looks awful—white-cheeked and shadow-eyed, and he's barely touched his sandwich. His hands are trembling on the steering wheel.

"Dad?" I say.

"Ummm?"

"I'm scared," I say. "So's Mum, and I bet Theo isn't exactly thrilled. But don't shut us out, Dad. Don't pretend it's not happening."

Dad's jaw clenches up. It makes him look like Nell.

"I'm worried too, of course I am. But I'm not *pretending* anything."

"So why didn't you go to the hospital straightaway? Why did it take you—"

He stops me with his hand. "Enough, Alice, all right? I've got Lara and Poppy to think of as well. I can't just leave everything at the drop of a hat."

I turn away. So that's what this is to him. His son's just had a transplant and he calls it "the drop of a hat."

My heart is pounding really hard. I need to calm down.

"It was a shock today," says Dad, finally.

"Yes," I say, staring out the window, though all I see is dark glass. "It was."

That's something we agree on, at least.

18

An hour later, we finally turn off the main road. Rain lashes against the windscreen, so it's hard to see up ahead, even with the wipers on full. When we reach the place where the road forks, Dad turns right for Nell's. We get a glimpse of the track in the headlights.

"Oh heck!" says Dad, slowing down. "I'd forgotten what happens here when it rains."

The track now looks more like a river. Luckily, it's not that deep yet. But the water has carried stones with it; our tires crunch as we drive. Then the wheels start to spin.

"This isn't good," Dad says, changing gear. We slither side-ways. The hedge scratches against the side of the car.

"That's my paintwork ruined," Dad says.

"Stop, then. We can walk from here."

"No, I'll drop you at the gate."

"Aren't you coming to see Nell?"

He shakes his head. "Not tonight."

I notice his hands gripping the steering wheel again. His jaw is still clenched just like Nell's. It makes me think of the telling-off I've got coming to me. But it won't be the worst thing that's happened today, not by a mile.

Just before the gate, we slide to a halt.

"I'll keep the headlights on so you can see your way in," Dad says.

So I get out and slam the door. Wrapping my arms around myself, I start walking. It's slippery underfoot. The water comes up over my trainers and soaks the bottoms of my jeans. I don't care. I'm just glad to be out of the car.

Up ahead, as always, Nell's lights are on. The name "Darkling Cottage" is just about visible through the rain. I'm almost relieved to see it.

"Aha, the wanderer returns."

Nell's on the other side of the gate, coat hood up, torch in hand. She doesn't sound as cross as I expected. Borage sticks his muzzle through the bars and tries to lick me. I reach over to pat him. Nell doesn't move. Then, shielding her eyes, she squints up the lane at the reversing car.

"Where's your mother going?" she says.

"That was Dad who dropped me off."

She squares her shoulders. Her face changes so she looks . . . what? . . . Upset? Angry? It's hard to tell.

"So he was at the hospital, eh?" Nell says. "Wonders never cease."

"Of course he was there. Theo's really sick." Though I don't like her saying this because I know what she means.

Nell sighs. "Well, I hope David copes with it better this time."

This time?

She doesn't say any more. But, lifting the gate latch, she lets me in.

Just before dawn, there's a noise at my window. It sounds like someone's pelting it with gravel. For a sleepy second, I think it's Flo come to find me, but the noise keeps on. It's at the other window too, and I realize it's just raining really hard. Pulling the blankets over my head, I try to go back to sleep. But my brain's so full of hospitals that in the end I give up and get out of bed to go and make some tea.

Out on the stairs, it's pitch-dark. One hand on the rail, I feel my way down the steep attic stairs. Something makes me pause on the first-floor landing. The passage to Nell's room looks darker than ever. Quickly, I move on. I've not gone three steps when there's a noise.

I stop.

All I hear now is the rain outside. I take two more steps down.

Stop.

The noise is behind me. I retrace my steps back up to the landing. The noise stops. I stand very still. Even my own breathing sounds loud.

It starts again. It's a person crying. In Nell's bedroom. *What do I do? Check she's all right? Go back to bed?* The crying goes on. It's not the heaving, sobbing sort that makes your nose run. It sounds really sad. And it feels wrong to just stand here, eavesdropping. Taking a deep breath, I go toward her door. The crying gets louder. Raising my hand to knock, I hesitate.

Should I do this?

I'm not at home now, and the person crying isn't Mum or Theo. Nell probably doesn't want my help. She might get angry. Or embarrassed. I don't know what to do.

There's a draft on my feet. It's coming from the end of the passage. A light is on down there too, as if a door's been left open. I really ought to go and switch it off. But when I realize which door it is, goose bumps run up my arms.

On tiptoes, I creep along the passage to the point where the wall curves. Two steps down and I'm facing a door—not a red curtain this time, because that's been pushed aside. The door's not locked, either. It's half open and the light from inside spills out into the passage. I should turn off the light and go. But something stops me. Directly behind me is that empty bedroom, the one that might've been Dad's. Perhaps all his stuff is now stored in this little room. It wouldn't hurt to have a look.

I slip inside. The room itself is tiny—not much more than a cupboard—yet it's absolutely jam-packed. Trunks, suitcases, rolled-up carpets all tower above me in great, musty piles. It's like being in a junk shop. It can't possibly all be Dad's stuff.

The trunks have names written on them:

"Campbell," mostly, though a few say "Waterhouse," which isn't a name I know. Up against the wall are stacks of books spotted with mold. Everything has dust on it, even the floor, which is so dirty there are footprints just inside the door.

Stepping farther in, I stub my toe on something hard. *Very* hard. The pain shoots through my foot and brings tears to my eyes. Then I see what I've walked into: it's the leg of a table piled high with boxes and books, and so big it almost fills the whole room. Everything, it seems, is on top of this table.

Except for two things.

Underneath it, just out of reach, is a pot with a screw-on lid. Nearer to me is a pretty wooden box about the size of a shoebox, which I imagine is full of old necklaces and rings. There's a lock on the front; a small key pokes out of it.

Crouching down, I lift out the box and balance it on my lap. The key's stiff. A few wiggles and it grates, then clicks open. I lift the lid. It's not a jewelry box. Inside are envelopes—letters, I suppose, though I've no idea whose. They look really old, like when you stain paper with a tea bag. I take one out for a better look.

"What ON EARTH?"

My hand freezes. Nell's right behind me.

"I was just . . ."

"Come away from those things AT ONCE!"

I stand up slowly, putting the letters back into the box and setting the whole thing down on the floor. My heart's leaping all over the place.

"The weather woke me up so I came downstairs and I heard . . ."

She glares at me. "That will do."

I stare at my feet. There's blood on my toe.

"You have no right to be in here snooping around," says Nell.

"I only meant to turn out the—"

"You were snooping! I won't have it in my house! Do you understand?"

My eyes start to fill up.

"*Do* you?"

"Yes," I say.

Nell takes a long breath through her nose. She's shaking.

"Go to bed," she says.

I duck past her and race back to my room. Once the door's shut, I lean against it, heart still hammering. Nell's already cross with me for going to London. Now I've gone and made things worse.

19

"I don't believe I'm doing very well, am I?" Nell says at breakfast.

I look up from my toast. This isn't the telling-off I was expecting.

"First you roam the countryside at night, then you sneak off to London without a word to anyone. You've made it clear you're not happy here," she says.

"I'm okay."

"Are you? When your school phoned yesterday to tell me you were absent, I spoke to your Head of Year, a Mr. . . ."

"Jennings," I say, feeling my stomach start to knot.

"Yes, Mr. Jennings. It was rather awkward, Alice. He said he wasn't sure you'd settled in very well. And that you'd not done your maths or French homework."

"Only once! I *always* do homework—well, normally." I stare miserably at my plate. I don't know what normal is anymore.

"And," Nell continues, "he thought there'd been an issue between you and another girl."

"Oh. That." What she means is Ella. And I'm not sure what

to say, especially as the "issue" she's talking about is Darkling Wood.

"Are you not happy at school? Is that it?" asks Nell.

"School's all right. But I do miss my best friend from home, Lexie."

"Is there no one else to be friends with?"

"Well," I say, thinking of Max. "There are some nice people."

"And what's the problem with homework?"

I shrug. "I didn't feel like doing it."

"Then that's not good enough," says Nell, quite sharply. "Mr. Jennings mentioned your attitude. He's sure it's due to the stress you're under, but you'd still better watch yourself, young lady."

My shoulders tense up. Now we're getting to the telling-off part.

"Perhaps I should call your mother and tell her it's not working out for you here," Nell says.

"Honestly, I'm okay," I say quickly.

What I mean is the alternative is worse. I can't go home or to Lexie's house. Which leaves Dad. No way am I going to stay with him and Lara, not even if he invites me. Which he hasn't.

"I'm not cut out for teenagers," says Nell. She's got that far-off look like she gets when she talks about the trees. "I didn't do so well with my own two."

At least, I think that's what she says, but then the telephone starts ringing. We both rush for it. Nell gets there first.

"Campbell residence," she says.

I hover, ready to grab the phone if it's Mum.

"I'm aware it's raining, Mr. Giles," Nell says, tight-lipped. "I'm also *well* aware that you should have been here half an hour ago."

I go back to my breakfast, glad the call isn't for me after all. My head's still full of flashing red lights and the panic in Mum's face, and I'm struggling to unthink it. I've certainly had my fill of hospitals for a while. I wonder if Dad's gone back to London today. Or whether he's had his fill too.

Out in the hallway Nell's voice gets louder. "So you won't be here on Monday either?" She sighs angrily.

"Tuesday, then?"

As I listen, my stomach starts to sink because I've guessed Mr. Giles must be the tree surgeon.

"I'll expect you Tuesday morning, eight o'clock sharp. Are we clear, Mr. Giles?"

Nell slams the phone down and storms back into the kitchen. Borage hides under the table, putting his chin on my knee.

"This is ridiculous," she says, sloshing water into the kettle. "If that man doesn't turn up on Tuesday, I'll do the job myself."

"Cut down the trees, you mean?" I say.

"Of course I mean cutting down the trees!" she snaps.

So it's finally happening. A man is coming to cut down Darkling Wood. I feel suddenly, painfully sad—and something else too, a sort of dread deep inside me.

"Look at us!" Nell gestures at the ceiling lights, which as usual are on. "We're living in semi-darkness here! We might as well exist in a cave!"

"But it's winter," I say. "At home we've had our lights on a lot too."

She's not listening. "And that's without considering the damage those roots are doing to this house. I spoke to the insurance company yesterday; they won't even insure me any-more. So if a tree falls on the house or if my walls start to crack

113

from subsidence, there's no backup, no money to cover the costs."

"But—"

"Don't you see? Those woods have made this house worthless." She's turned her back on me to stare out the window. Her shoulders are trembling. But I don't think she's crying . . . *or is she?*

"Nell?"

"They've got to go." Her voice is matter-of-fact. "I don't care if I have to use my bare hands. I want my house to be safe and light."

She turns around. There aren't any tears. Her face is bone dry.

"Those trees are coming down. And that's final." The kettle boils. Nell makes her coffee, scraping her spoon against the cup. It sets my teeth on edge.

"That Traveler girl you saw the other day in the woods."

I put down my toast.

"You did tell her to clear off, didn't you?"

"Um . . . sort of . . ."

"Well, she'd better not be anywhere near the place when Mr. Giles comes. I mean it—there'll be falling trees. It'll be dangerous."

Under the table, I cross my fingers. "If I see her, I'll tell her. She might still be around, climbing the trees or something."

"She'd better not be climbing my trees AT ALL!" cries Nell, slamming down her cup with such force it makes me jump. "She'll get herself killed!"

Nell's wrong. There's no way Flo would fall—it's almost like she was born to climb trees. But I can't say this, not without admitting I'm friends with the girl who's trespassing in her woods.

Nell takes a deep breath. "The sooner the wood goes, the better."

Yet I can't imagine this place without the trees all around it. I can't picture Flo anywhere else either. And I think of just how quiet it feels out there in the woods. Fairies or not, it's a special place.

"Can't Mr. Giles just ... I dunno ... trim the branches back?" I say.

Nell glares at me. "*Trim?* He's a tree surgeon, not a hairdresser! Good grief, child, you can't trim roots!"

"I just don't see why you have to cut down the whole wood, that's all," I say.

Nell blinks slowly. She takes a slow breath like she's trying to stay calm. It's obvious what she thinks of my suggestion.

"Perhaps I will speak to your mother," she says. "See if we can get someone to collect you."

My stomach plummets. "I'm not going to Dad's. So don't ask him."

"There must be someone else who'll have you."

"There isn't. You're it."

We stare at each other for a very long moment.

"We'll leave it a few days, then," she says. "But today, young lady, you're grounded."

"What?!" I sit bolt upright. "All day?"

"Absolutely. No running off anywhere. I want you here where I can keep an eye on you."

"But I have to ..." I stop.

"Yes?" says Nell, interested. "What do you have to do, Alice? Because if there's a problem, I will call your mother."

I pick up my toast again. "Forget it. It's nothing."

All day, Nell works outside taking down the fence that

separates the woods from the garden. And I sit at the kitchen table, trying to read or do school stuff. But really I'm thinking about Flo. Yesterday proved I can't always help Theo or Mum, but perhaps there's something we can do about Darkling Wood. Not the fairies business, I mean something real and practical. Sensible. There must be another way to make the trees safe without cutting everything down.

There's another thing too, niggling in the background like toothache. Normally I'm not one for superstitions, but I can't shake off what Flo said about revenge.

Darkling Cottage
Saturday, 16 November 1918

Dearest Alfred,

The War Office might believe you are "missing, believed killed," but I believe you're on your way home. After all, no one's yet proved that you're not.

Papa also thinks you're still alive. At breakfast, he said a dead person's spirit often returns to a place they loved (our beech tree, perhaps?) but as he'd seen no sign of yours, you must still be alive. I confess I like the idea, though I'd rather you weren't dead at all. But Mama said she found our talk most unhelpful. She's been busy writing to your regiment for information, so now there's even less paper to use.

On the subject of letters, I set out directly after breakfast to post yours. Well, you know how news travels in Bexton. Standing in the post office queue, I lost count of the glances that out of pity couldn't meet mine. At least when I reached Mr. Crabtree at the counter, I was a tiny bit prepared. As I passed him your letter, his eyebrows went skyward and his hand hovered over the stamps. I held my breath. You see, Alfred, suddenly that letter meant everything. I was desperate for him to send it, just like he'd sent my other letters. I couldn't bear to see his hesitation or the doubt on his face. It felt like the difference between believing and giving up. So when Mr. Crabtree finally stamped the envelope, I'm afraid I did sob with relief.

As you know, I'm not one for tears in public, so I was very glad to leave the village behind me. Marching straight up the hill, I didn't stop until I reached the woods. Oh, Alfred! What a sight awaited me! Hovering beneath our tree like a dragonfly was one of the tiny creatures. As I approached, she flew toward me, coming so close I saw the startling blue of her eyes. Then she touched my tear-stained face—first the left cheek, then the right—before retreating back under the tree. From there she carried on watching me. And when I touched my own cheek, the tears had all dried. I felt calmer too, as if a knot inside me had worked loose.

That peace didn't last.

Hurtling down the path came the black-and-white dog from the farm. Not far behind was Mr. Glossop with his gun under his arm. Two dead rabbits hung from his shoulder. Seeing me, he whistled the dog to his side.

My first thought was for the creature under our tree. You know what Mr. Glossop's like—he's hardly civil to people, never mind something as unusual as this. He'd want to hunt it down. Kill it. Show it to the men in the pub. So, politely but firmly, I asked Mr. Glossop to turn back.

He didn't take kindly to getting orders from a girl—in fact he went very red in the face. It took all my courage not to step aside. But he barged past me anyway, and in his haste walked straight into a low-hanging branch. The force of it felled him. He landed with a thump, dropping his gun, then he lay on the ground clutching his forehead. It was terribly hard not to laugh, for he did look jolly funny.

I know I should've offered my help, but the fact was I couldn't get near him for his dog snarling and snapping. Anyway, Mr. Glossop was soon on his feet again. Pulling his cap down to hide his face, he stormed off with his gun through the undergrowth.

By now, the little green creature had vanished. There was something odd about that tree branch too. It didn't look that low. It wasn't even really near the path. So how Mr. Glossop came to walk right into it, I don't know. It was as if the wood—or something in it—had played a trick on him.

Back at home, Papa was on the lawn with his camera. I went over to tell him about Mr. Glossop, but before I had a chance even to speak Papa made me stand very still. My expression was just marvelous, he said, and he wanted to take my picture. Don't laugh!

Later Papa showed me the finished photograph and he had captured me well, right down to the tangles in my hair. And yet, I didn't look like a person who'd just caught a poacher. I looked like a girl who'd seen magic.

So I tried to tell Papa what I'd seen today. I'd met a creature with wings, I said, and somehow it'd lifted my sorry spirits. He listened until I'd finished, then he patted my hand and said how lovely that I was a dreamer just like him.

Yet it happened, Alfred, and I know you believe me. The proof is that photograph; it's there in my face.

Your devoted sister

118

20

Sunday, 17 November

Something's seriously up with Nell this morning. She's storming about the place before it's even light. I pull the covers over my head, but when I hear her talking on the phone, I immediately think it's to Mum. Quickly putting on jeans and a jumper, I go downstairs. Nell's in the hallway, phone tucked under her chin.

"Yes, every single blasted one," she's saying. "Right back in their original places. Can you believe it, Mr. Giles, they've even nailed the posts back together!"

Nell notices me hovering. She gestures toward the kitchen like there's something she wants me to see. I don't know what she's on about: everything looks normal in here. The table is covered in papers and coffee cups. And Borage, the great lazy lump, is still in his bed by the Aga.

"What's going on, boy?" I say, crouching down to rub his ears.

He thumps his tail. *Not much, by the looks of it.* Taking the kettle to the sink to fill it, I gaze blearily out the window. Today I need to find Flo. There must be something we can do to save the woods—something that doesn't involve fairies.

"Seen it, have you?" says Nell, coming into the kitchen.

"Huh?"

She joins me at the window. "That fence I took down yesterday—d'you see where it is now?"

Wiping off the condensation, I peer through the glass. I'm still not sure what she's on about. The fence that separates the garden from the wood looks like it always does—wooden posts, wooden rails.

Except . . . hang on . . . yesterday Nell took the fence down. I watched from the window and saw the posts she'd dug up lying in a big heap. It took her ages. Now they're all back in the ground.

"Who did it?" I ask.

"I've no idea," says Nell. "Someone's playing tricks on me."

My heart starts to thump.

Flo said this would happen, didn't she? She said there'd be more hold-ups, more delays. And someone or *something* has messed with Nell's fence, all right. It'll take her ages to dig those posts up again.

I feel a chill creeping over me. Flo called them *tricks*. She said they were a warning to Nell not to cut down Darkling Wood. If she ignores them and goes ahead, the fairies will take revenge, and I've a nasty suspicion who their target will be.

Us.

"I'm not still grounded, am I?" I say to Nell.

"What?" Nell looks surprised. Her mind's clearly on other things. "No."

Grabbing my coat, I race out the door. I need to find Flo. Fast.

I head straight to the woods. The birds are quiet, as if they know something's wrong. Even the trees look grim. It's hard not to think of what they'll look like next week, hacked to pieces on the ground. There's no sign of Flo in the usual places, not even a footprint. I just hope she's not still cross with me over last time, and that business with the note I found in the tree.

At the edge of the wood, I turn left toward Glossop's Farm, where the Travelers are camped. If Flo won't come to me, I'll have to go to her. It's a steep climb up the hill. At the very top the ground falls away toward a line of trees. Stopping to catch my breath, I see the crooked chimney of a house, a rooftop with tiles missing, and rows of smashed-in windows. So this is Glossop's Farm. Someone must've lived here once; now, though, it's bleak and empty. Perhaps the building wasn't safe to live in. Perhaps there were problems with tree roots here too.

A dog barks nearby. The sound's coming from some parked-up vehicles just beyond the farmhouse. There's an old horsebox done out for living in, buses, brightly colored trucks, a couple of caravans. If this is the Travelers' camp, then Flo must be down there too.

I get as far as the line of trees before something knocks me flying. I fall hard on my bum. Next thing, I'm pinned to the ground by a massive black dog.

"Off, Raven!" someone shouts. "Get off!"

A hand grabs the animal and yanks it away. Shakily, I sit up. Two feet wrapped in plastic bags appear next to me.

"You all right, chick?" says a woman.

I try out my legs and arms. I don't seem to be bleeding.

"I think so," I say.

"Can you stand up?" says the woman.

She's got a bit of rope around the dog now. He's big and squat with a massive head. And he's still a bit too interested in me.

"Keep the dog back," I say.

I'm not scared of dogs, but this monster makes me very nervous. No wonder Flo doesn't like them. Slowly, I get up.

"What you wanting here, anyway?" says the woman, now she sees I'm not bleeding to death.

"I'm looking for a girl," I say.

"Oh aye. A school friend, are you? What's your name?"

"Alice," I say.

"You're the new student, aren't you?" the woman says, folding her arms. "Aye, she's mentioned you."

"Has she?" I try to be polite, but all the time I'm glancing over her shoulder. "Could you tell Flo that I'm here, please? I really need to see her."

"Flo?"

The woman hasn't moved. She's not exactly friendly, not like my mum, who insists on hugging all my friends. And I'm getting the sense now that maybe she doesn't know who I'm talking about.

"Yes, Flo—short for Florence. Nell ... I mean, my grandmother ... said Flo lived here at the Travelers' camp."

The woman catches this name too. "Nell? Nell Campbell? That crazy old bint who owns Darkling Wood?"

I shuffle my feet. It's like being at the village shop again.

"Yes," I say. "And that's why I need to see Flo."

The woman's face drops. "Your grandma hasn't got the go-ahead to cut the wood down, has she? The council haven't said yes?"

"They don't need to, apparently. The work starts on Tuesday."

"Flaming heck! It's criminal, that is, to cut down such an

old bit of woodland! Those trees should be protected!" the woman cries. "I can't believe no one's put a stop to it!"

According to Flo, the fairies are trying. Though I don't say this.

"So is she around?" I ask again. "Nell said . . ."

"Then your grandma's got her facts wrong, hasn't she?" The woman's voice has an edge to it now. "You won't find any *Flo* here in our camp."

The dog starts growling again. The woman steps nearer.

"Look," I say, trying to sound braver than I feel. "I don't want the wood cut down either."

Then someone shouts, "Mum! Stop being so *embarrassing*!"

The woman spins around. Two people step down from the horsebox and come toward us—a man, and a girl wearing the brightest striped tights I've ever seen. She looks like . . . no, wait . . . she *is* Ella from school. I'm completely thrown.

"Oh." Ella stops when she sees me. "It's you."

"Who's this, then, love?" says the man, who I suppose is her dad.

"Someone from school," says Ella.

I think of those posters she put up last week and feel my insides shrink.

"Aha! Nice to meet you." Her dad sticks out a grubby hand.

Awkwardly, I shake it.

"Here, Del," says the woman who must be Ella's mum. "You know you've just shaken hands with Nell Campbell's granddaughter, don't you?"

The man looks at me, then at his hand, which he wipes on the back of his jeans.

"You tell your grandmother we're going to fight her," he

says, not so friendly now. "Whenever she starts destroying that wood, we'll be there. You tell her."

"It's starting Tuesday," says the woman.

"This Tuesday? In two days' time? Hell's bells!"

"I don't want it to happen either," I say. "I'm just trying to find my friend Flo so we can do something about it."

The three of them look at me, stony-faced. It's no good. They don't believe me.

"You'd better go," the woman says. "Your grandmother will be wondering where you are."

I feel their eyes on me all the way back up the hill. What bothers me more, though, is that I still haven't found Flo.

21

Back in the woods, something rustles high above my head. I look up. See a flash of red and white between the branches. It's Flo. Thank goodness.

"There you are!" I shout up to her. "Where've you been? I've been looking for you!"

"I'm here now," she says, "so stop fussing."

"I'm not fussing!"

She's clearly not cross with me because her face is one big grin. I grin back. I'm just relieved I've found her.

Flo moves down the tree like most people climb stairs. She stops about halfway and sits on a branch.

I look up, shielding my eyes so I can see her better.

"The tree surgeon's coming on Tuesday to start work, Flo. And I've been thinking, you're right—these woods are amazing. We need to do what we can to save them."

Flo shuffles farther down the tree. I see her properly now, and she's gone a bit pale.

"Tuesday's the day?" she says, no longer grinning.

"Yes. So we need a plan. I can speak to Nell, though I'm not exactly in her good books," I say, ticking it off on my fingers. "And perhaps you could ..."

Flo interrupts. "What happened between you and Nell?"

"We had a fight. I went off to London to see my brother without telling anyone and I shouldn't have done. Anyway, so on Tuesday ..."

"I told you there'd be trouble," Flo cuts in again. "It's what happens when the little people aren't happy."

"You think the *fairies* made me fall out with Nell?"

"Yes. And the other problems she's been having."

"Mr. Giles didn't make it because of the bad weather," I say, but then think of the fence that was somehow put back up again.

She's right, isn't she? This is happening.

"So," says Flo. "We need a plan, do we?"

I nod. Whatever may or may not be going on with fairies, I need to be practical. "There's lots we could do—make banners, put up posters, stuff like that. We could put locks on the gates to the wood, and ..." Seeing Flo's face, I stop. "What's wrong?"

"You haven't listened, have you?" says Flo.

"We're back to fairies again, aren't we?" I say with a sigh.

"I've told you, Alice. The fairies will fight for Darkling Wood, but they need you to believe in them to give their magic more strength."

I fold my arms. "And I've told you—you can't make me believe in something that's not real."

"It would be easier if you stopped looking at me like I'm completely loopy," she says. "You know what the fairies want you to do."

This is stupid.

"All right." I throw my arms out wide and yell at the top of my voice, "Hey, everyone! I believe in fairies! I really, really do!"

There's rustling in the bushes. A terrified blackbird swoops past.

I look up at Flo. "There. Happy now?"

"Don't be silly," she says, sounding cross again. "You have to actually mean it. The fairies are very sensitive; they'll know you're lying. When you finally do believe, you'll be able to see them. That's why you saw nothing the other day when you looked through the fairy door."

It was just a hole in a tree, I think; that's why I didn't see anything. But there is ... I don't know ... *something* about Darkling Wood.

"Okay, I admit these woods are pretty special," I say. "The way they make you feel at peace; it *is* sort of magical."

Flo looks pleased. "That's better."

This is mad. *She's* mad. But it's not like my ideas are works of genius. And we're running out of time.

"Trust me, Alice," she says. "This is urgent. We need to work on getting you to believe in fairies."

"How, exactly?"

"Trust me," she says again. I groan.

"Tell me about your father," she says.

Bam. Just like that. It throws me completely. "What's that got to do with fairies?"

The corners of Flo's mouth twitch. I think she's going to laugh.

"Stop being so ... *practical* for a moment, and tell me."

Near Flo's feet I catch sight of the fairy door where she left that stupid note, the one she thought would help. Turned out my idea to visit Theo didn't help much either. I suppose that puts us both out of luck today.

I tuck my hair behind my ears. "Okay, but there's not much to tell. Dad got his dream job in Devon designing houses made of wood. But it wasn't a dream for Mum, so we stayed behind and they split up. We saw Dad some weekends and holidays. Then Theo got sick and bit by bit we saw even less of him. Dad lives with Lara now—she's his girlfriend, and they've got a baby called Poppy. That's it. My dad in a nutshell."

Flo looks horrified.

"Your father stopped seeing you when your brother got sick?" she says. "How could he do that?"

My heart sinks a bit. She's right. *How could he?*

"I don't know."

"Have you seen him since?" Flo asks.

"I saw him at the hospital the other day. He brought me back here afterward—well, he dropped me outside."

"Nell is his mother, isn't she? Didn't he want to pay her a visit?"

Flo has these funny little phrases. "No, he didn't want to *pay her a visit.*"

"Why not?"

"I don't know. He doesn't come here. He never brought us here when we were little or anything."

Flo goes quiet.

I shoot her a look. "What?"

"Does he know about the trees being cut down?" Flo says.

"Who?"

She sighs. "Your father, Alice, wakey wakey!"

"What d'you mean?"

"Your grandmother is fixated on the trees, and your father never comes here. Maybe there's a connection."

"All I know is he's scared about Theo. He freaked out at the hospital—so did I."

Flo frowns. "That doesn't explain why he wouldn't visit his own mother."

I don't know what to think.

Certainly Nell doesn't want Dad to come here. It might be because Mr. Giles is about to start cutting down the trees. But then it might not. I also don't know why Nell was crying last night or what it was in that little room she didn't want me to touch. Maybe these things aren't connected.

Or maybe they are.

All this talking has made me more confused than ever. Yet one thing is clear: we have to save the wood. I still don't believe in fairies, not really, but I can't shake off the dread I feel when Flo mentions revenge. In my head it's all mixed up, so it almost seems like the woods and Theo are linked and if we save one, then we'll be saving the other. It's mad. But I can't help thinking it.

"Alice! Alice! Are you there?"

I go still. Someone's calling me. It's coming from over by the gate. There it is again. It's Nell.

My stomach drops.

Theo.

"I'll have to go," I say to Flo.

Nell's voice is clearer now. "Alice! Quickly! Your mother's on the phone!"

I run.

And as I do, just for a second, something pale green like a butterfly flits alongside me though the trees.

129

22

"Now, Alice," Mum says.

I sink down onto the bottom step of the stairs. This is her "bad news" voice. I've heard it lots these past few weeks: it turns me to ice.

"Your grandmother says she's struggling with you, especially after your trip to London. I think we need to talk."

"Oh . . . right."

This isn't about Theo. The relief is so massive, I almost laugh.

"What's Nell been saying?" I ask.

"She says you keep going off without telling her."

"Don't worry, I'm not going to turn up in London again."

"Glad to hear it," says Mum. "It wasn't one of your better ideas."

"Suppose not."

"The thing is, Alice, your grandmother thinks you're not happy there with her."

"Really?" I pick at a loose bit of paint on the wall. "She's actually noticed?"

"What d'you mean?"

I look over my shoulder just to check that Nell hasn't followed me into the house. She hasn't; she's still hammering away at something outside.

"Honestly, Mum, she's got this amazing wood right outside her back door and she's getting rid of it because she says it's not safe and it'll ruin her house. But the trees are really old. Really beautiful, only she doesn't see it like that."

I picture Mum rubbing her forehead as she listens.

"Nell didn't say anything about the wood, sweetie. She was concerned about you coming to London, yes. But she also said you've been wandering around her place at night."

"She didn't mention the climbing-trees thing? She went mental when she thought I'd been doing that."

"No, this wasn't about climbing trees. She said you've been looking through her belongings."

"Oh." I swallow. "Right."

"Is that true?"

I get my nail right under a flake of paint and pull.

"Alice?"

I don't know quite how to put it. Okay, so I shouldn't have gone in that room without asking. But why's Nell keeping all that stuff locked away, anyway? And why was she crying in the night? She never asks about Theo either—but why would she, when she doesn't even speak to her own son?

I don't suppose Mum will want to hear all this, so I choose my words carefully.

"It's not that I don't like staying here," I say. "I'm okay with it if I can't come home. I've made some friends too."

"That's good."

"But this place is a bit . . . well . . . strange."

"Strange isn't necessarily bad," Mum says. "Think how boring life would be if we all ate the same food, drove the same cars, watched the same TV series."

"There isn't even a TV here," I say. "But I'd happily eat different food. Nell's cooking is disgusting."

"Your grandmother might seem a tough cookie, Alice. But she strikes me as someone who's had her fair share of hard times."

"She's weird."

Mum sighs. "It's not like you to be difficult, sweetie. We're all finding this hard, aren't we?"

I nod. I'm picking the paint faster.

"Alice? Are you listening to me?"

"Sorry."

"Just try to be good, will you?"

"I *am* trying."

"Then try harder, please." Mum sounds tired. "I've got enough going on here at the hospital."

"What's happened now?" I ask, alarmed.

"Oh . . . just your dad. He said he'd visit today and he hasn't showed up. Theo keeps asking when he's coming, and I don't know what to tell him. Your father owes me big-time for this one."

I remember how Dad's hands shook as he drove back from London. He was scared. Sounds like he still is. I know what that feels like, but he's the grown-up here, and he shouldn't be letting Theo down.

Mum starts up again. "So what I *don't* need today is drama from you."

"Me?"

Dad not showing up isn't my fault. My eyes sting with tears.

And for the first time in my life, I put the phone down on Mum. Then I remember I didn't ask after Theo, which makes me feel bad all over again.

This is Nell's fault. She's phoned Mum behind my back like some sneaky teacher at school. Why the heck didn't she just speak to me?

I storm outside to find Nell. She's at the side of the house, taking down the fence again. She's wearing a big tool belt around her hips, and the way she's swinging her hammer around makes me think of that funny word to do with sword fights: *swashbuckling*.

"Why did you phone my mum?" I ask.

"Not now, I'm busy," she says, waving me away. I don't move.

"You grounded me yesterday—that was enough," I say. "You didn't have to go and worry Mum."

Nell's hammer stops mid-swing. "Oh, so it's my fault, is it? I'm the one who's running away without telling people, and sneaking around in the night?"

I fold my arms across my chest. I can feel my heart beating fast.

"You didn't have to speak to her," I say.

"*You* didn't have to run away," she snaps back.

"I wasn't running away. I was visiting Theo."

"And what were you doing in the little bedroom upstairs?" Nell says. "It looked like prying to me."

"I wasn't—"

She laughs in disbelief. "I caught you red-handed, Alice! Or am I seeing things?"

"I couldn't sleep, all right?"

"You were going through private, personal things that

133

don't concern you. And for your information, young lady, your mother isn't the only person coping with other issues."

Hard times, Mum said. I stare at the ground.

"Are we finished?" Nell says. "Because I've got work to do. You'll remember he's coming on Tuesday?"

"Who, Dad?"

It's a total slip: I've no idea why I say it.

"Good grief, child, no!" Nell cries. "Why on earth would I want him here? I meant Mr. Giles, the tree surgeon."

"Oh, *him.*"

Mr. Giles or Dad—the thought of either makes my heart crash to the ground.

I escape back to the woods, but Flo's nowhere to be seen. I call her name but all it does is panic the birds. I feel hopeless. I don't see how anyone's going to save Darkling Wood at this rate. This whole situation feels like it's growing roots itself. It's not just about protecting the foundations of the house or letting more light in. If Flo's right, then this could also be about Dad. And if she's right about that, then maybe she's right about the fairies too.

I don't know. I just don't know.

Last night's poor sleep is catching up with me. I'm tired. Fed up. I want to go home. Leaning back against the beech tree, I close my eyes. Sunlight falls on my face. Behind my eyelids the colors start to spin. I feel lighter. Calmer.

Perhaps Flo really does see fairies. Standing here now, I can almost understand why. This wood is full of strangeness. Even the sunlight becomes something different as it falls through the trees.

But then.

Fairies. I mean, *really*?

When I open my eyes everything is gold sparkles. It might just be dizziness. Or it might be something magical. I can't be sure.

One blink and it's gone.

Darkling Cottage
Sunday, 17 November 1918

Dearest Alfred,

    There are fairies in Darkling Wood.

    Yes, you did read that last sentence correctly. I have proof at last, so now people should jolly well believe me!

    It wasn't easy to get my hands on Papa's camera. All morning we sat in the library, Papa reading his magazine on "psychic matters," and me not settling to anything. In the end I got Anna to make up the fire until it was positively roasting, which promptly sent Papa to sleep. At last I was able to sneak away.

    A few days ago, Papa's photography things were moved upstairs into Maisie's room on account of Mama hating the mess. To keep out the light, a thick curtain has been hung across the door, and inside an enormous table has been set up, which almost fills the little room. It was on this table that the camera sat, as if waiting for me! I'd seen Papa load it with six or eight glass plates: I took just one. Then tiptoeing back downstairs and past the library, I fetched my coat.

Crikey, it was cold outside. Frost still hung thickly in the trees, and the ground beneath my feet was so hard it sounded almost hollow. At first, I couldn't set the blasted camera up. It was simply a few buttons and clips but my fingers had gone so numb with cold it took forever, though having watched Papa, I knew how it was done. After a couple more tries, I got the back open and the plate properly into place with the big spring firmly behind it. Once the camera made a whirring sound, I knew it was ready.

At first there was nothing to photograph. Putting the camera down, I sat back against the tree, wrapped my arms around my knees and waited. My feet grew cold. I imagined warming pans and woolen socks until it became impossible to think of anything else.

Quite suddenly, the grass to my left quivered. A tiny leg appeared. Then came another, followed by a golden-haired head. Standing before me was that same winged creature, or one just like her. I held my breath in delight.

This time the creature didn't seem quite solid, almost as if she was made of mist or moonlight. She hovered so close I saw every fold in her clothes. And yet I saw through her too. It was most peculiar. Then she reached out. And, oh Alfred, she touched my feet!

Instantly my toes tingled and were warm. Then came the strangest sensation—it felt sharper, clearer than the calmness from before. It was as if my head had been swept quite clean. I confess I forgot EVERYTHING. All that mattered was this moment, this pinprick of time, sitting here with a fairy in my sights. What a wonderful photograph it would make!

Moving oh so slowly so as not to scare her, I lifted the

camera off the ground and held it in my hand. With the other, I moved the lens till the creature wasn't blurry. It was so hard to keep steady. At last I pressed the button.

Click.

The creature vanished.

It was like waking from a dream I didn't want to end. Yet I knew this wasn't a dream; it had really happened. All I had to do now was develop the picture, but until then the glass plate must stay inside the camera, out of the light.

Back at home, Papa was still asleep, so I tiptoed upstairs and got to work. First, I set up trays of solution like I'd seen him do. Then, once the curtain was pulled across and the door shut, I opened the camera. Just as Papa did, I put the plate into the solution. And waited—I had to guess as to how long.

After a while an outline appeared. I'd remembered how Papa had put the red light on—the "safe light," he called it, because it didn't damage the picture. I did it now, and goodness, how my hands shook!

What can I say? The image came out perfectly. There she was, Alfred. Up against the tree trunk, she looked tiny, like a flower or a fleck of light. I imagined how Mama would say it was dust on the lens, but to me it was clear as day. She was, most definitely, my fairy.

What happened next was an accident. In my excitement I tripped over the table leg, sending trays, bottles, and tongs flying. The clatter woke Papa, who appeared in the doorway, demanding to know WHAT THE BLUE BLAZES was going on. Then he saw the negative. And do you know, he laughed out loud!

We did the last bit of developing together. I think perhaps

Papa was even more excited than I was. He believed in that picture, Alfred. Like me, he wanted the fairies to be real.

We waited until after tea to show Mama. I was nervous—and with good reason. When I put the picture in her lap, she barely looked at it. Her eyes were drilling into me.

What right did I have to take Papa's equipment? she asked. Proper young ladies filled their time doing useful, charitable things. They didn't spend all day in the woods, climbing trees.

I didn't see what the fuss was about. No one ever died from climbing trees, I said, and was promptly told to hush my mouth. Mama insisted I was too old for all this silliness. And I was certainly too old to be taking pictures of my dolls.

Well! It wasn't a doll in my picture, Alfred. On that, Papa and I were in firm agreement.

Papa says he knows a man with a special interest in pictures like mine. He's going to invite him to Darkling, which has cheered me rather, even if Mama thinks it's all nonsense. You see everything's been so bleak of late, and this picture of mine has given us all something else to think about. It feels like a glimmer of hope.

Your ever-loving sister

23

Monday, 18 November

I'm in Mr. Jennings's office with the door closed. My hands are
sweating. I don't like these teacher talks.

"I understand this is a difficult time for you, Alice," he
says. "But while you're attending this school, you're Ferndean's
responsibility. We really can't have you missing school and not
completing homework."

I keep my eyes on the carpet.

"Is there anything we can do to help?" he says. "A session
with our counselor, maybe?"

I shake my head. *Not more talking.*

"Then ..." He pauses. "How about we let you off doing
homework for a week or so? You're clearly struggling to keep
up with it."

Again I shake my head.

"I'm trying to help you, Alice. Yours are special circumstances, and being exempt from doing homework might take
the pressure off," says Mr. Jennings.

"Thank you, sir, but I'm fine," I say.

His "special circumstances" idea makes me uncomfortable.

No one used those words at my other school. No one treated me differently, and I didn't want them to either.

This time I meet Mr. Jennings's eye. "I'd rather do my homework just like everyone else, sir."

"Are you sure?"

I hesitate. There's bound to be homework today, and I still have to catch up on the lessons I missed last Friday. But I hate being singled out because of Theo. It makes it harder to forget what's happening, and sometimes I want to try.

"Totally sure, sir."

"Very well. From now on we'll expect your homework to be in on time. If it isn't, I'll be calling your grandmother again—and this time, I'll invite her in for a chat."

I get an image of Mr. Jennings, Nell, and me, all here in this room. It's not nice. Not one bit.

By break time I've got English homework and more words to learn for French. There's also a meeting about to start in our tutor room. Through the door I see bright green "SAVE DARKLING WOOD" posters on the walls.

"Come on," says Max, taking my elbow and trying to steer me past. "I'll buy you a hot chocolate."

He's being sweet, I know, but what's the point in hiding from Ella when I want to save Darkling Wood too? And though I'm beginning to think there might be fairies there, Ella's protest feels more concrete. More real. I want to take part in it, if she'll have me.

"Thanks for the offer, but I'm going in," I say to Max. "Coming?"

"I'd rather get a hot chocolate."

As he leaves, I open the classroom door. Down at the front, Ella's handing out little green badges saying "SAVE DARKLING WOOD." It's a genius idea. Trust her to think of badges.

"Can I have one, please?" I say, joining the group stood around her.

Ella stiffens. The other students move aside. A space forms around me.

"What d'you want, Alice?" Ella says.

"I want to save the wood. Just like you do."

Ella does a big weary sigh. "Why would you want that when it's *your* grandmother, who *you're* staying with, who's cutting the trees down?"

It's a fair point. Nell and I have spoken about the trees, and I've told her I don't think they should come down. That's all she knows, though. And it should stay that way until tomorrow. I can't risk her grounding me again, or worse, sending me to Dad's.

"I know those woods now. I feel sort of connected," I say. "Every morning, I look out my bedroom window and see them. And every night, I walk through them on my way home from school."

"You've only been there a week," Ella reminds me.

"Yes, and it feels like forever."

I look at the other students here. There's got to be twenty of them at least, each wearing a bright green badge on their blazer.

"Have any of you ever been to Darkling Wood?" I ask.

They glance at each other. One girl wearing glasses raises her hand.

"Do the rest of you even know where it is?"

More glances. Ella rolls her eyes. "What's your point, Alice?"

"My point is that most of you are protesting about a place you don't even know. So what if I've only been here a week? At least I know what Darkling Wood looks like, what it smells like. It's not just a wood, it's an amazing place. It's . . . magical!"

I must've got a bit carried away, because they're all staring at me now. A couple of year sevens actually have their mouths open.

"You're right, I guess. It is kind of magical," says Ella warily.

I nod. "A friend of mine really believes it is. She says if we destroy the wood then the fairies who live there will take revenge on us."

A few people start sniggering. Now I have said too much. It's stupid to think they'd believe in fairies: I mean, I'm only *maybe* coming around to the idea. But when I glance at Ella, I see her face is lit up, and she takes me to one side, while the rest of the group starts chatting.

She says in a whisper, "My mum thinks there are fairies in Darkling Wood."

"Has she ever seen any?"

Ella shakes her head. "No. She believes they're there, but says only people with a special gift can actually see fairies."

My stomach does a swoop. Flo said something similar, didn't she? Or at least she said the fairies had chosen me for a reason. Might this *be* the reason? It's hard to think so—I don't exactly feel like someone with a special gift.

Yet the thought stays with me. And as the room fills with more excited chatter, I feel my mood lifting. Ella's group is organized and thorough. When she calls for quiet, they all listen like I bet they never do in class.

"The work on Darkling Wood starts tomorrow. We, ladies and gents, need to be there to make a . . . well . . . let's call it a *nuisance* of ourselves."

"That won't be hard!" someone chips in. Everyone laughs.

"So, how about we meet tomorrow morning in Bexton village square, say eight-fifteen, sharp?" Ella says. "Oh, and be prepared to get muddy."

A girl with blond hair says, "What about school?"

"Skip school," says Ella. People share nervous looks.

"I mean it," Ella says again. "We all have to skip school."

I don't think they'd quite signed up for that.

"Can't we do the protest *after* school?" someone says.

Ella sighs. "Look, what's the point in doing a protest to an empty lane? We need to be there when the work starts. We need to get in the way."

"But I'll never convince my mum to drop me in Bexton rather than here," says another girl.

A ripple goes through the group. People shake their heads. A few unpin their badges. More make their way to the door. As the room steadily empties, Ella frowns but stays calm.

"I'll be there tomorrow morning, with or without your support," she says to the last few students as they leave.

I'm the only person left. I'm not going anywhere.

"Here," Ella says, passing me a badge.

I pin it on my blazer and smile. She smiles back.

"Looks like it's down to you and me," she says.

And the fairies, I think, because try as I might, I can't forget their part in this.

Max is waiting for me outside the classroom. He hands me a cup of hot chocolate that's still warm.

"You star!" I say. "Thanks so much!"

Max does a little bow. "Not at all."

He grins in that way that makes his eyes twinkle. As if I've not got enough going on right now, I think I'm getting a crush on him.

After break it's history. Straightaway Mrs. Copeland talks about last week's homework, and how today's lesson will be based on it.

"So get your notes out, please," she says. "We'll do this in register order."

"What homework?" I say to Max. I picture Mr. Jennings dialing Nell's number and cover my face with my hands.

"The homework set last Friday when you were ill," says Max.

"I wasn't ill," I say, moving my hands away. "I went to London to see my brother." I don't mention the being sick part.

"Oh. Okay. Well, we've all had to choose a person to base our project on."

I stare at him in panic.

"Hello? Anyone in there?" says Max, waving at me. "A person who was alive in 1918? Who was affected by the war ending?"

I nod. I remember the project. "But what are we doing now in register order?"

"We've got to talk for a minute on the person we've chosen and why."

My mouth goes dry. "Oh."

"Campbell" is near the top of the register, so I know I'm going to get called soon. What's worse is the five students going before me all do brilliantly. One boy's chosen his great-great-grandfather, another boy talks about a football player for the local 1918 team. Someone else does the old head teacher for this school. By the next two I've stopped listening properly. All I hear is how confident they sound and how many enthusiastic comments Mrs. Copeland makes.

Then it's my turn.

Mrs. Copeland sees the confusion on my face. "It's okay, Alice, I know you missed Friday's lesson, so you probably haven't done this, have you?"

"No, miss," I mutter.

"Do you have anyone in mind for your project?"

"No, miss."

Everyone's looking at me now.

"That's fine. Don't worry," says Mrs. Copeland.

"I'll catch up, miss," I say.

"You don't have to, Alice." She gives me a knowing look. That look says "exceptional circumstances." She doesn't know about my agreement with Mr. Jennings, it's obvious.

One of the back row boys says loudly, "That's not fair, miss. On Friday you told us we'd get a detention if we didn't do the homework."

Mrs. Copeland holds up her hand. "Alex, I think . . ."

"Yeah, miss," says someone else. "That's favoritism, that is."

A murmur goes around the classroom. I'm feeling really uncomfortable now. "I'll do it by next lesson, miss," I say.

The murmuring stops. Mrs. Copeland moves on down the register. And my brain starts whirring because I've not got the foggiest idea who to base my project on, or where to even start.

24

At a quarter to six, I give up. With no Internet to use for research, this history project has got me stumped. I can't do it. I can't do anything. To make the point, I throw my exercise book across the kitchen and thump my head down on the table. I don't know anything about anyone alive in 1918, let alone someone remotely interesting.

It's dark outside. Next time the sun comes up will be the day the trees are cut down. There was no sign of Flo on the way home from school. All I can do is trust the fairies to work their magic, even though it still sounds a bit mad. At least we've got Ella's plan as backup. Or perhaps that should be the other way around.

And then there's Nell.

To be honest, I'm starting to feel shifty. All she wants to do is protect her house from tree roots, and I'm here, a guest in her home, plotting against her.

Tomorrow there'll be a protest about it too, never mind what the fairies might do. I think it's probably fair to warn her.

At seven o'clock, I knock on the library door.

"Supper's ready!"

I've found enough in Nell's cupboards to make us a pasta bake. When we've eaten, I'll tell her about tomorrow.

Nell comes into the kitchen, Borage at her heels.

"It's sweltering in here!" she says. Leaning over the sink, she opens a window. There's no mention of the table laid with her best matching plates or the pasta bake bubbling in the middle.

"I used the hot shelf of the Aga," I say, because I'm quite pleased with how my first-ever attempt to cook in Nell's stove has turned out.

"You didn't use the microwave?"

"No, just the Aga."

She looks shocked. Genuinely.

"Try some." I put a spoonful on her plate. The bottom layer's burnt and the carrots are still crunchy, but the rest looks pretty good.

Nell sniffs at it. "What's in it?"

"Onions, leeks, carrots."

She blows on it, then takes the tiniest forkful, pulling faces because it's still too hot. The way she wrinkles up her nose makes her look so like Theo. I can't believe I've not noticed it before.

"Is it all right?" I ask.

"It's rather nice," she says.

"I wanted to cook you something, you know, for a change."

"Oh," says Nell. "And there I was thinking you were trying to butter me up."

I fiddle with the pepper pot. Nell moves it to one side, out of my reach. "What's this really about, Alice?" she says.

147

"Umm . . ." I clear my throat. "It's about the woods tomorrow."

Nell narrows her eyes, first at me, then at what's behind me, hanging on the back of my chair.

"Save Darkling Wood," she murmurs.

"What?" Then I guess what she's spotted. On the back of the chair is my school blazer. The bright green badge is still attached.

I clear my throat. "Nell, I need to tell you . . ."

She's not listening. Her attention's been caught by Borage now, who's sat bolt upright in his bed. There's a noise outside, a car engine. Headlights sweep down the lane. The dog starts barking. Nell gets to her feet.

"Who the devil can that be?" she says, grabbing the torch off its hook.

Holding on to Borage, I follow her to the front door. It's pitch-black out there. The torch beam picks up a number plate, a silver-gray bumper, a person getting out the driver's door. With a jolt, I recognize the car.

It can't be, I think. *No one told me.*

Nell's hand covers her mouth.

"Oh gracious!" she says. For a second, I think she's actually going to shut the front door.

"I won't come in," says Dad.

"I'm not inviting you in," says Nell.

Borage is still growling; no one bothers telling him to shut up.

"What brings you here, David?" asks Nell.

I can't believe she's being so cool, not when my heart's about to burst from my chest.

"It's Theo, isn't it?" I say, pushing past her. "What's going on?"

Dad holds his hands up. "Whoa, Alice! Slow down! Theo's okay."

"Is he? Are you sure? You've been to see him?"

"I spoke to your mum a couple of hours ago. He's okay, honestly. Not brilliant, but okay."

"Good!" I gasp, clutching my chest in relief. Next to me, Nell sighs very quietly. It's the sound a frightened person makes when they start to feel a bit less scared. Yet that can't be right. My grandmother's not scared of anything. Or anyone.

"So why are you here?" says Nell. "And please be brief. You're letting out all the heat, keeping this door open." Actually, the kitchen's the only warm room. But I don't think this is about heating. It's about getting rid of Dad as fast as possible.

He glances my way, then at Borage, who's standing in front of me like a giant, furry wall. Dad takes a nervous step back.

"Alice," he says, "your mother's worried about you."

"I'm fine," I say a bit too quickly.

"She's fine," agrees Nell. I'm not sure why she's sticking up for me, not after the conversation we've just had. I'm sure she just wants Dad to leave.

Dad shrugs. "Your mum doesn't think so. She said you put the phone down on her yesterday."

"Oh."

"And if *she* thinks something's up with you, then, you know, maybe she's right."

I frown at him. Since when did he start agreeing with Mum?

"So," Dad continues, "she's asked me to take you to Devon to stay with me. You'll have to kip on the sofa, I'm afraid. What d'you think?"

A heavy feeling lands in the pit of my stomach.

"I can't."

Dad looks uneasy. As he rubs his jaw, it makes a scratchy, bristly sound. "I know it's not perfect, but Lara wants to meet you properly, and you've still not seen Poppy, have you? She's grown so much."

Poppy. I wish they'd called her something awful.

"Well, this is all very charming . . . ," says Nell, starting to close the front door. Dad sticks his foot in the way.

"I'm not going," I say.

"Come on, Alice. You've been enough of a burden on your grandmother."

"How very thoughtful of you," says Nell.

But I don't want to sleep on his sofa. I don't want to wake up in his house with his new family and see him loving other people more than he loves us. And then there's Flo. And Ella. And tomorrow. I can't leave now.

"I've got a history project to hand in at school tomorrow and I've put loads of work into it," I say, though the lie makes me wince.

"Don't make this any harder for me, Alice," Dad says.

"Hard for *you*?" Nell snorts. "That's so typical of you, David. Always putting your own feelings first."

Dad rolls his eyes. "I didn't come here to fight." There's a silence.

Then Nell says, "Just go."

I think she means both of us. Dad moves back from the door. He reaches into his pocket and jangles the car keys.

"You've got ten minutes to get your things. I'll wait for you in the car."

"I'm not coming."

"Ten minutes," says Dad, like he's not heard me.

Nell turns away. Calling Borage to her side, she heads back to the kitchen.

"Dad," I say into the darkness. "I mean it. I'm staying here."

Turning up his coat collar, he doesn't look around. And in that moment he seems farther away than ever.

25

Yet twenty minutes later, Dad's back. It's me that answers the door to him; Nell's shut herself up in the library.

"The car won't start," he says through gritted teeth. Behind him, the silver car hasn't moved an inch.

Dad holds up a smart-looking phone. "My mobile won't work down here either. Can I use the landline?"

I'm not sure I should let him in. But it'll only take a minute, and then he'll be gone again.

"The phone's there," I say, pointing to the spindly table at the foot of the stairs.

"Same as always," he says. "Nothing's changed here." I'm guessing he doesn't know about tomorrow yet, when the whole feel of this place will change for good.

He puts his mobile and car keys on the table, then makes his calls. I sit on the bottom stair hugging my knees. It seems the garage can't come out until tomorrow. When Dad finally puts the phone down, he rubs his hands over his face.

"What are you going to do?" I ask.

"Sleep in the car, I suppose." He picks up the phone again. "I'm just calling Lara to let her know where I am."

This is one conversation I don't need to hear. I get up just as the library door opens.

"What's going on?" says Nell.

As she sees Dad, her face turns to ice.

"His car's broken down. He's only using the phone," I say, then feel cross because it sounds like I'm defending him and I'm not.

There's a click as Dad puts the phone down.

"That car can't stay where it is," says Nell.

"And how do you propose I move it?" says Dad.

"I don't care. Just make sure it's gone by the morning," Nell snaps. "I can't have it blocking the front gate."

Her hands are back on her hips again, like earlier when she was on the phone to Mr. Giles.

"What's happening tomorrow that's so important?" Dad asks.

"Nothing for you to ruin," she says.

But it's starting to dawn on me: that's exactly *it*. Dad being here will hold things up. The fairies are still working their mischief. They're still trying to save the wood. And a car blocking the front gate so no workmen can get in tomorrow is a pretty good attempt.

No one speaks. Nell folds her arms. Dad looks like he's going to say something, then changes his mind and picks up his keys. He slams the front door behind him.

Nell glares at the space where Dad was. Then she turns to me. "Your father is not welcome in this house."

I don't speak.

"He forfeited that right twenty-one years ago when he interfered in things he didn't understand. And now you're about to do the same with this 'Save Darkling Wood' nonsense."

"It's not nonsense," I say. "Please, Nell, will you listen for a minute?"

She shakes her head. "I'm too tired for this. Just don't make the same mistake your father made. Remember whose woods those are, young lady, and keep your nose out of what doesn't concern you."

It's too late. This isn't just about me anymore. It's bigger than that—bigger even than the woods. It's about my family and why they're at each other's throats.

Whatever Dad did all those years ago, Nell's still mad as hell about it. She's clearly not about to share it either, for she turns on her heel and goes back to the library. Another door slams shut.

The house falls quiet again. But it's not peaceful anymore; the air prickles with bad feeling. I go back to the kitchen, where at least it's warm.

"I wish people were as straightforward as dogs," I say to Borage as I feed him cold pasta bake from my fingers.

I clear the rest of the food away. Wash up. Sweep the floor. Just like at home, doing stuff calms me down. But then I remember my history homework, and my shoulders tense. There's nothing else for it; I'll have to give it another go.

I rescue my book from where it fell beside the bin and sit at the table. The blank pages stare back at me. Head in hands, I make myself think of the film we watched in class: the marching soldiers, the hats in the air, all that *hope* for something better. But it's pointless. All I see is Ella's colorful mind map, and I think how I haven't even got a pencil case because it's in my bag and that's still with a ticket collector in London. It's no use pretending I can do this; I can't.

All that's left is to go to bed. Crossing the hall, I see Dad's left his mobile on the table. I pick it up. It's a very nice phone. New, slim. Full of charge. Really I should take it out to him, even though it won't work down here.

I hesitate. Looking at the solid black battery symbol, I remember there *is* a place where phones work. It's no help to Dad, who's stuck outside, but I'm inside and a quick call to my best friend might cheer me up.

Assuming Nell's still in the library, I race upstairs and switch on the lights. And even then it's still dark enough that Dad's phone glows. At the end of the passage, the door to the little room is shut. Instead of the red curtain pulled neatly across, it hangs untidily to one side, as if someone in a hurry has been here and forgot to draw it closed.

I dial Lexie's number from memory. Or what I think is her number. It clicks onto an answer phone that's not hers. I try again. The same thing happens. I try her landline. No answer. Perhaps she's out having fun with Bethany Cox.

I hear something else. Holding the phone away from my ear, I listen.

Someone's crying.

Just like before, it's coming from Nell's bedroom. This time I don't hesitate—I knock.

"Go to bed, Alice," she says.

"Are you okay, though?"

She doesn't answer. I'm guessing she's upset about seeing Dad again. After twenty-one years of not getting along it must be a massive shock. I wait. Wait a bit more. The sobbing goes quiet. Her bedroom light clicks off and I hear the rustling of bedclothes, a cough. It doesn't seem right to stay and listen.

As I head for the attic, I've still got Dad's phone. I bet it's full of pictures of Lara and Poppy and I don't trust myself not to look. So I go back downstairs and take it out to him in his car. He's not there, though, so I follow the path that runs down the side of the house; he's got to be here somewhere.

It's a clear night. The stars are out and the grass is frosted over. Everything is quiet—even the woods—as if it's all holding its breath. Dad's leaning on what's left of the fence, looking at the trees.

"Oh, thanks," he says when I give him his phone.

He goes quiet again for a very long time. It's like he's in a sort of dream.

"When I was a kid I thought there were fairies in this wood," he says finally. "I never saw any, mind you, though it didn't stop me looking."

I shiver a little. Pull my jumper sleeves down over my hands to warm them. It's strange hearing Dad speak like this. He's usually so logical and precise. He likes to make things, plan things. Or he did. Now there's another "Dad" who I don't know very well. He's scared, he gets things wrong, lets people down. And he says he believes in fairies.

"Why did you believe in fairies, Dad?" I ask, because today Ella said her mum did too, and I'm wondering now if it's not just Flo who thinks fairies exist.

He smiles. "They were magical, you know? A mystery. They weren't like frogs or tadpoles. You couldn't catch one and keep it in a jar. Sometimes I wonder if this is the only magic place still left—here in these three acres."

I don't say anything. He doesn't know about tomorrow and I'm not going to tell him. That's up to Nell.

"I've never told you, have I, about when you were born?" he says, turning to me.

"In the car, on the way back from a New Year's party. Yes, you've told me. So's Mum, plenty of times."

"But not the Chime Child part?"

"The *what*?"

"You were born at about three in the morning . . ."

"Yes," I say. "I know."

". . . which makes you a Chime Child. The myth says a child born between midnight on Friday and cockcrow on a Saturday—the chime hours—has second sight. It means you can see fairies and spirits."

I laugh. Then stop. I get a fluttering feeling in my chest.

Is this the reason the fairies have chosen me? Is this the special gift Ella was talking about today?

"Are you joking?" I say to Dad.

One look tells me he's not. His foot on the lower rail, he's staring dreamily into the woods again. I feel the hairs lift on the back of my neck. And as I follow his gaze I see two small green shapes dart between the trees. This time I'm sure I'm not imagining it.

Darkling Cottage
Monday, 18 November 1918

Dearest Alfred,

 Today a Very Important Person came to visit. You'll never guess who, so don't even try! All Papa said beforehand was that this person was an expert, by which I assumed he meant in photography.

Yet who should arrive? None other than the world-famous author of the Sherlock Holmes stories! Yes, he was HERE in Darkling Cottage! It was thrilling and confusing, but most of all really rather terrifying.

It turns out Papa knew Sir Arthur Conan Doyle through his regiment. He'd also read Sir Arthur's articles on psychic matters in that magazine he gets called The Strand, *and so decided to contact him for advice. When Sir Arthur received Papa's telegram, he jumped straight in his motor car—a fine shiny green one with a fold-down roof—and drove the hundred miles to our house without stopping. We received the telegram to say he was coming just half an hour before he arrived.*

Imagine the panic! And yes, there was a moment before opening it when we thought the telegram brought news of you. Once we'd recovered, Mama insisted I change into my best blue frock. I didn't know what was wrong with the one I was wearing; I could brush off most of the mud. But you know how particular Mama is. She didn't believe my picture one bit, and if Sir Arthur were about to find us out as fakes, then we'd jolly well be tidy ones!

Our visitor arrived just after two. With him was a man called Mr. Robinson who, it turns out, really is an expert in photography. Yet all eyes were on Sir Arthur. Have I told you how tall he is? Honestly, his head touched the light fittings! Papa showed our guests to the library. Mama and I followed. Anna and Mrs. Cotter were also invited to meet the great man himself, and to see my picture. It hit me then that this wasn't a secret anymore, not even just between

Papa and me. Now a whole roomful of people would be in on it, which I confess only added to my nerves.

Before he'd even seen the picture, Sir Arthur said he'd like to ask me some questions. His hands were tucked in his waistcoat pockets—I almost imagined it was Sherlock Holmes about to interview me. Papa looked on, awestruck.

Sir Arthur started by asking what I'd seen in the wood. I didn't know quite what to say at first, especially with other people in the room, all there to listen. But Sir Arthur was very kind and patient, and said did I know children were more in tune with the spirit world than adults? Mama cut in to say actually I'd had the flu at the time. Mrs. Cotter and Anna shared a look. But dear Papa patted my arm and explained I was a Chime Child, which Sir Arthur agreed might have a bearing on my case.

Next he was shown the photograph. On picking it up off the table, Sir Arthur first held it at arm's length. Then he brought it very close to his face. He peered at every single inch of it, top to bottom. It was most nerve-racking to watch.

By the time he invited Mr. Robinson to inspect the picture himself, I felt positively sick. Eyebrows went up. Notes were made. Then heads close together, they spoke in low, excited voices. I was desperate to know what they were saying.

Finally, Sir Arthur joined us at the fireside. He cleared his throat in a way that made me more nervous, if that was possible. It was his and Mr. Robinson's opinion, he said, that the picture wasn't a fake. There was a clear sense of movement in what was a single-exposure shot. Strange too, he said, how the fairy's figure cast no shadow.

Papa seized my hands. We both started laughing like lunatics. Now, Alfred, I knew that picture wasn't fake: I'd taken it myself. But to hear someone else say so was the finest thing. He believed me! Sir Arthur Conan Doyle believed me!

And how did Mama take the news? She looked uncomfortable, but thankfully she busied herself arranging coffee cups and cake. Not that I wanted cake—I was too stirred up for anything!

After forcing down what refreshments I could manage, Sir Arthur insisted I take him "to the very spot" where I'd seen fairies: I desperately hoped we'd see one. The sun was low in the sky, a proper winter sun that dazzled between the tree trunks. It made me think of sunsets, and for a moment I felt sad, like I'd reached the end of a brilliant story. Only nothing had ended, Alfred, in fact it was just beginning.

Even so I was jolly relieved when a fairy did appear. Not only that, she hovered exactly at our FAVORITE place, where the tree grows strangely. When I pointed her out to Sir Arthur, he seemed unable to see her himself, yet he didn't think I was pretending. He just said it proved I was a Chime Child.

He said another thing too—this'll interest you. That strange O-shaped branch? Well, apparently it's a FAIRY DOOR, a very magical spot where fairies pass between our world and theirs. No wonder we picked that beech tree above all the others.

There's more.

Beside me, Sir Arthur suddenly flinched. His hands went to his head and he ducked as if warding off a blow. Then something hit me—doof!—right on the forehead. Another hit me on the arm. Then the leg. Then the shoulder. The ammunition, I realized, was vicious little pea-sized stones.

And the sniper?

My fairy, who was invisible to Sir Arthur but who I could see all too clearly. She was glaring right at us. Other fairies had joined her on the branch, or, should I say, at the fairy door. And let me tell you, scowling and glowering at us, they looked awfully fierce. It was most unsettling. I felt ashamed that my fairy should be unfriendly, and confused as to why she should be so now. They stayed there too, arms folded, staring down at us. It was we who retreated in the end.

Back at the house, Sir Arthur laughed it off. He called it typical fairy mischief and said it only made my case stronger. I don't know, Alfred. Those fairies didn't seem happy. Perhaps they just wanted to be left alone. The problem now is that Sir Arthur wants more photographs.

I'm beginning to wonder what on earth it is I've started.

More soon,
Your sister

26

Tuesday, 19 November

I think I saw fairies in the trees last night, yet this morning nothing's changed. There've been no last-minute phone calls, no cancellations, no more fairy mischief. Today's the day Darkling Wood gets cut down. All I can hope now is that Ella's protest works.

I can't face breakfast. There's no sign of Nell anywhere. Or Dad. I get my school books and pull on my coat just like normal. Today, though, I'll be heading down to Bexton village square to meet Ella, and the fact Dad's car is still blocking the driveway makes this easier because Nell can't give me a lift.

It's then I hear voices outside the kitchen window. The first is Nell's. "There's no mistake, David. I need you to move your car. Mr. Giles is coming this morning to start work on Darkling Wood. I'm having it cleared."

"Cleared?"

"That's right. It's being cut down. The whole three acres."

Silence.

Then Dad says something I can't hear, so, opening the

back door, I slip outside. They've moved around to the side of the house: I can't see them, but there's a crunching sound as someone paces up and down the gravel path.

Nell's voice is raised. "This is my house and my decision."

"But there must be a preservation order on those trees! They're hundreds of years old!"

"No, David, there isn't. I'm in the middle of nowhere out here. And they're a risk to the house. The insurance company says so."

"Rubbish! I'll check with the council myself."

"Go ahead," says Nell. "But you're not using my phone."

Dad spits out the words: "I can't believe you'd do it without telling me!"

"Tell you? Why would I tell you? We don't speak anymore, or have you conveniently forgotten that fact?"

"Then what are we doing now?"

Silence again.

"I just can't believe you'd do this," repeats Dad.

"The trees are going because their roots are threatening the house. If I don't remove them the insurance company won't cover me. Besides, the house is dark, the garden's dark. Nothing grows down here. We get no sun. I'm sick of living in the shadows."

"But that wood . . . that's my childhood . . . there, in Darkling Wood!"

Nell sighs heavily. "And what a childhood it was, eh? I should've had those trees down years ago. Then none of this would've happened."

"Those trees have been here longer than this house! They're meant to be there! There's magic in those woods!" Dad yells. "This is the stupidest thing I've EVER heard!"

"No, David, the stupidest thing was to take something that wasn't yours!" Nell shouts back.

Borage presses against my leg. He doesn't like shouting. Nor do I. It takes me right back to Mum and Dad and how even with my fingers in my ears I still heard them.

"How can you say that, after what *you* did?" Dad cries.

"Oh, don't be childish, David."

I don't think this is about the trees anymore. I creep right up to the corner of the house and peer around. Borage comes too. Dad and Nell are only a few feet away now.

"You did it without asking anyone," Dad says.

"It was done to help another family," Nell says. "I can't believe you don't realize that, especially now, with Theo."

I catch my breath. Nell—who never talks about her grandson—has mentioned Theo.

"But it wasn't Jacob's choice, it was yours!" says Dad. They're going too fast. I don't know anyone called Jacob.

"Yes," Nell says. "It was my choice. When your son recovers, maybe you'll understand."

"What if he doesn't?"

I don't mean to sob, but it comes out too loud. Nell and Dad both spin around. Borage leaps out from our hiding place, tail wagging.

"I've spoken to you before about prying," Nell says, and she's not talking to the dog.

I don't move.

"What are you arguing about? Who's Jacob?" I look from her to Dad and back again.

Dad groans.

Very firmly, Nell takes my arm and pushes me toward

the house. "Get to school, young lady, or I'll drag you there myself!"

I leave without another word, hot and churned up, and more confused than ever. Flo was right: there is a link between Nell and Dad's falling out and the woods. Though she's never mentioned a person called Jacob.

By the time I reach the village square, the church clock is showing half past eight. I'm late. There's no sign of Ella or anyone from school yet. I can't have missed her: I walked the usual way through the woods, so I'd have passed her if she'd been there.

I wait a bit longer. By 8:50 a.m., I'm close to tears. She's not coming. No one is. So much for Ella's smart badges and her big plans to make a nuisance. I feel stupid for thinking any of it would work. So when the bus for town pulls up, I get on and head for school. There's nothing more I can do.

By the time I reach Ferndean High, I've missed the first lesson entirely. The second lesson is history. Ella's not here.

"Where's Ella?" I whisper to Max.

"Ill, maybe?" he says. But I don't think either of us believes it.

It's obvious where she is. Somehow I missed her in Bexton this morning, and now I'm stuck here in class and she's at Darkling Wood saving the trees. I cuss myself for getting on that stupid school bus. Why didn't I just wait a bit longer? Why didn't I go back to the wood?

"Everything okay, Alice?" Mrs. Copeland asks as she leans in to check my homework.

"Yes, miss," I say, but I'm fidgety as anything.

"Why don't you take off your coat?" she says. Though I do as she says, I really can't sit still. Stupid, *stupid* me.

Mrs. Copeland skims my book. "Did you find someone to do your project on? Can I see your notes?"

"Ummm . . . I think they're here," I say, turning pages and pretending to look.

There is no history homework. Mrs. Copeland knows it and so do I. My face is burning. I'm such a rubbish liar.

Someone on the back row mutters "Detention" under their breath. Mrs. Copeland does her teacher glare; it goes quiet again.

"Let's talk after class," she says to me, and her look tells me she's spoken to Mr. Jennings. She knows the score.

Max lends me a pen and I write the date and learning objective from the board. The lesson starts, but I don't listen to a word of it. I can't stop picturing Nell's trees toppling to the ground. It makes my head hurt.

Then there's a knock at the door and Mr. Jennings comes in. Automatically people smooth their shirts down and tighten their ties, but he's not here to check our uniform. He goes straight to Mrs. Copeland. Dipping their heads, they talk quietly in that way teachers do, and I wonder if she's telling him about my homework. But then Mrs. Copeland looks at me, and her expression isn't angry; it's soft and kind. My legs turn instantly to water.

This isn't about homework. Something's happened to Theo. I feel my whole body go cold.

"Come with me please, Alice," Mr. Jennings says. His eyes flick left and right. "Bring your things, and a friend, if you like."

Suddenly I don't want to leave the room. I want the lesson

to keep going as if nothing's wrong. I'd rather be stuck here forever.

Max is already on his feet. He helps me stand up.

"Come on, Alice," he says, tucking his arm through mine.

We follow Mr. Jennings back to his office. By the time we get there, my teeth are chattering. Mr. Jennings shuts the door and offers Max and me seats, then perches on the edge of his desk.

"We've had a call from your mother," Mr. Jennings says. "She tried to contact your grandmother first but couldn't get a reply. I'm afraid things aren't too good at the hospital. Your brother's condition has deteriorated." His voice sounds distant. Like he's talking to another person in another room. My heart starts to beat very fast. Mr. Jennings offers me a tissue; I take it for something to do with my hands.

"You'll probably want to go home," Mr. Jennings says. "We'll get someone to collect you, shall we?"

"Who?" I say. "My dad's waiting for the garage to fix his car. It's blocking the driveway. No one can get in or out."

"My dad could pick you up and take you home," says Max. "He's working at Darkling Wood today. I'll try his mobile."

"*Your* dad?"

"Sure, if it'll help."

I picture the man in the luminous orange coat who was there making notes that day Flo and I hid from Nell. I stare at Max. "So . . . wait . . . your dad's the tree surgeon?"

"Yup."

"Why didn't you tell me?"

Max shrugs a shoulder. "I thought . . . I dunno . . . it might complicate things."

I grit my teeth. Right now I'd like to shake him, but before

I can stop myself, tears roll down my face. Everything is jumbled up. It shouldn't be happening like this.

I did what Flo wanted me to. I believed in fairies—I mean, I must have, because those green shapes in the trees last night were fairies, I'm sure of it. She said if I believed, it would make their magic stronger. She said they could save the wood.

If the wood was saved, there'd be no more bad luck. No more fairy tricks like fences being taken apart or cars breaking down. No more talk of revenge. That's what I believed.

But it's like we've skipped a stage. Things have gone too fast. We're already at the terrible part: cut down the wood, Flo said, and the fairies won't just work magic anymore, they'll be out for revenge.

And now it's happening. This is the worst, most awful luck. It's the thing I've feared more than anything. Theo is getting sicker. But it's not meant to be like this.

I breathe in. Breathe out.

There must still be something we can do.

27

Mr. Giles's jeep smells of petrol. He drives faster than Nell, taking corners like a rally driver. By the time we reach the top of the track, I feel sick. But amazingly we've made it home in less than twenty minutes.

"Nearly there," he says. "Hold on tight."

Wheels spinning, he zooms down the last bit of track. It's the steepest part. My stomach feels like it's up near my ears. I grip the dashboard and squeeze my eyes shut. We lurch left, then right. The whole jeep judders. As we take the last bend, Mr. Giles slams on the brakes.

"What the . . . ?"

My eyes fly open. I brace myself. We stop just in time. Parked on the track is an old horsebox. Another few feet and we'd have gone into the back of it. Mr. Giles scratches his head. Beeps his horn. Neither makes anything happen.

We're stuck.

"Where's that come from?" says Mr. Giles.

"I don't know."

The lane is blocked. Which means no one, not even a tree

surgeon, can reach the house. And with no tree surgeon, no trees will be cut down. Darkling Wood stays.

This is the fairies' work. It has to be.

It's hard to think straight when my mind's so full of Theo. Yet I get the tingly feeling that something magical is happening.

"I'll drop you here, is that all right?" Mr. Giles says.

"You're not starting on the trees today?" I ask, just to be sure.

Mr. Giles shakes his head. "Not when I can't even get near the place. I've plenty more work to keep me busy today."

Once I'm out of the jeep, I feel strange and light-headed. This is it. This is what we wanted. What the fairies wanted. Darkling Wood is saved—at least for today. The magic was strong enough after all.

Squeezing past the horsebox, I recognize the little curtains at the windows. It's where Ella lives. My heart does a skip. The others from school might've chickened out, but not Ella. She kept her word. And she's got her mum and dad involved too.

Wow, Ella, I think. Just WOW!

Perhaps the fairies played a part in that too, I don't know. It makes me want to burst into tears again.

Then, up ahead, I see Nell. She's talking to Ella. Behind them, just inside the gate, is Dad's car. It hasn't moved.

It can't move. Not until the garage mechanic fixes it. I miss a breath.

Oh no. This isn't good. We need the car to get to Theo. We have to be able to get out of here. To drive to London. The protest has to move.

I run.

Ella spots me first.

"Hey!" she says. "You made it! What d'you think? Reckon any tree surgeons can get through?"

From this angle it's even more obvious. The horsebox completely fills the track. It's not parked, it's *wedged* between the hedges. It's not going anywhere.

Nell turns to me. "You've got some explaining to do, my girl! You knew about this, didn't you?"

"Not exactly."

"What does *that* mean? And why aren't you at school?"

"It's Theo," I say. "Mum phoned the school. He's worse."

Nell's hand goes to her mouth. She looks smaller, like the fight's suddenly gone out of her. I turn to Ella.

"I'm sorry," I say. "But we have to get out. Or at least get to the garage."

Ella looks shocked too. "I'll speak to my dad."

She disappears inside the horsebox just as a man in a white van pulls up behind. "Get a shift on, will you?" he shouts out his window. "I'm here to fix a car."

I look for Nell, but she's gone. Moments later, she reappears at the side of the house with Dad. They go to the front door and she lets him inside, then she comes back to me.

"He's just using the phone to call the hospital," she says, seeing the question on my face.

I don't really care about their stupid argument, not now.

"The garage man's here," I say.

"And about time!"

Squaring her shoulders, she's big again. She strides up to the horsebox and bangs on the side door with her fist.

"It's no use hiding in there!" she says.

Almost straightaway, the door opens and Ella comes out with both her parents. Her dad looks taller today, more serious. Borage stands like a barrier in front of Nell.

"With or without a preservation order, it's still murder to

cut down those trees," says Ella's dad, folding his arms. "We're not moving until we've talked some sense into you."

I glance across at Nell. Straight-backed, gray-eyed, she stares back at him.

"Save your hippie nonsense for those who'll listen," she says.

"We knew the wood was coming down today." Ella's mum jabs a finger at Nell. "And it's time *you* listened, lady."

"How news travels," Nell mutters, and glares at me. I look away. I wish Dad would hurry up on the phone.

"Those woods are famous around here, Mrs. Campbell," says Ella's mum. "And not just because of you. The fairies live there, and have done for centuries."

I look back at Nell.

She does a cough. A half laugh. "My dear, that's rubbish. *Utter* rubbish."

Ella's mother smiles. "There's stories about Darkling Wood that could turn your blood," she says. "If you cut down those trees, the fairies'll be after you with their bad magic. And who'd want to bring that on themselves, eh?"

Not me, I think, a shiver going right down my backbone.

Nell holds up her hand. "That's enough! Now will you move?"

Ella's dad doesn't shift.

Nor does Nell, though her voice gets louder. "That car's needed," she says, pointing to Dad's. "Now move!" Arms folded, Ella's parents lean against the horsebox. They're going nowhere. Ella looks uncomfortable now, and farther up the track, the garage man presses his horn. Still no one moves. At this rate we'll be here tomorrow.

"Please," I say, over Nell's shoulder. "My brother's sick, and—"

"Don't tell these *people* our business!" Nell cries. They're not just "people." They're Ella's mum and dad here to save the wood. But now things have changed and we need to get to the hospital. I just wish everyone would hurry up. Even Dad's phone call is taking forever.

"I'm calling the police," says Nell. "They'll get this track cleared in no time."

I look at her in disbelief.

"Nell, just explain why we need to get out!" I cry. Ella tugs her mum's sleeve. She knows about Theo from school—or bits of it. But Nell's glare is now fixed on the Travelers. She's locked into battle and she can't back down. It's just how she is with Dad.

"Please," I say to Ella and her parents. "We need you to move. My brother's very sick and we have to get to London to the hospital. It's an emergency."

Ella's parents stop leaning against the horsebox and straighten up.

"My dad's car needs fixing first and we're in a hurry, so, please, could you move? The tree surgeon's already gone. He won't be back today."

"All right," says Ella's dad. "We'll let the garage man through."

"Thanks," I say.

"Though I'm warning you," he says to Nell. "This isn't over. We'll be back, and with more people next time."

Within half an hour Dad's car is fixed. But the news from the hospital is bad. Theo is doing very poorly, and though they're trying different drugs, the next few hours will be critical.

We saved Darkling Wood, I tell myself, so now that the fairies are happy, maybe our luck will change. I don't want to think about tomorrow, when Mr. Giles will be back. It's this moment I need to focus on. My little brother needs every single bit of good luck there is—and he needs it today, not tomorrow.

Dad gets in the car and starts it up. Going around to the other side, I open the passenger door.

"What are you doing?" he says as I slide into my seat.

"Coming with you."

"No, you're not."

"Oh yes, I am."

Dad turns the car engine off. He looks exhausted.

"Alice, Theo's in intensive care. It's just me who needs to go."

"Mum called *me* at school. She must want *me* to come too."

Dad sighs heavily. "No, Alice. She called the school because she couldn't get hold of me or Nell. This is 'parents only' stuff for now."

"Parents only? What does *that* mean? And when did you start caring?"

"Look, I need to go," he says. "We'll talk later, okay?" Then I notice his hands. They're trembling really badly. His voice sounds shaky too.

"You've done so much for your brother. You should be proud," Dad says. "But it's okay to be scared. And you and I, we're terrified, aren't we?"

I swallow and nod.

"Only one of us needs to face that hospital, Alice. And it's time I stopped being scared and started being more of a dad."

There's plenty I want to say to him. But I can't argue, because he's right.

28

Back inside the house, Nell's waiting. I know I'm in trouble. Yet she doesn't shout or yell or go all spiky. She simply gets up from the kitchen table and beckons me to follow.

"I want to show you something—properly this time," she says.

Upstairs, it seems darker than ever. We go to the end of the passage, then down the two steps that take us to the door behind the curtain. Unlocking the room, Nell flicks a switch on the wall. Light dazzles from a bare bulb strung with cobwebs. I've been bursting to search this place. Now, though, I hang back in the doorway as Nell pushes a cardboard box and some books to one side. She reaches underneath the table, groaning and twisting her arm until she's got what she's looking for.

"This," she says, straightening up, "is what it's all about."

She's holding the jar that I couldn't reach the other day. Seeing it properly now, it's actually a bit boring looking. I can't help but feel a little disappointed.

"Your father took this without asking," Nell says. "That's why we don't speak anymore."

"I don't get it. I mean, if he took it, why's it here and not with him?"

"He took what was *inside* it—twenty-one years ago." I stare at the jar. It's pottery with a metal lid and Nell holds it in front of her like a gift. As I go to take it, she whips it away like she can't quite let it go after all.

"What was inside?" I'm guessing money or jewelry. It must have been something big for her and Dad to fall out like that.

"Jacob," she says.

I dip my head. I don't think I've heard her properly.

"Jacob?"

Nell tuts. "Your father hasn't even told you that much, has he?"

Actually, neither of them would tell me anything when I asked this morning.

"He's your father's younger brother," she says.

"Dad hasn't got a brother." I look at Nell. Those steely gray eyes. "Has he?"

"He hasn't now, no. Jacob died when he was eleven. Your father was seventeen at the time."

"But he can't . . . I mean . . ." I stop, mouth open in shock.

"I'm sorry you've had to find out like this."

My own dad never mentioned he had a *brother*. There's so much of him I don't know about. And now there's another stranger in our family—Jacob—who, I'm finding out, was my uncle.

Nell tucks the jar under her arm. "Let's see," she says, and pulls out a box from the piles of stuff on top of the table. "No, not that one." She gets another one, rummages through, and pulls out a book that's covered in dusty cardboard. It's an old photograph album. I crane my neck for a look.

"That's Jacob," Nell says, pointing to a picture a couple of pages in. The photo is of a boy with thick blond hair, hanging upside down from a tree. He's wearing a striped jumper that looks like it's shrunk, and one of his front teeth is missing. It's a sweet, happy photo that makes me smile and go watery-eyed at the same time.

Then it comes back to me, what she said in the kitchen that day when she wanted to send me to Dad's: *I didn't do so well with my own two.* She must've been thinking about Jacob.

"How did Jacob die?" I ask.

Nell takes a breath. "He was out in the woods climbing a tree with your father when he slipped. The fall broke his neck."

I look at the picture again. It doesn't seem so sweet now, just really sad. He's the boy who never grew up to be some-one's dad, or to be my uncle, and Theo's. And that tree that he's hanging from—I wonder if that branch is part of Flo's fairy door, or whether it's just a trick of the light. Perhaps, like Dad, Jacob believed in fairies too.

"Oh," I say, "oh." So this is why Nell didn't want me to climb trees.

Tears fill my eyes, then spill down my face. An even more terrible thought hits me: by saying Jacob *slipped,* does she really mean something else, something ten times more awful?

"It was an accident, wasn't it?" I ask.

"Yes, it was. I don't blame your father, not for that. They'd climbed that tree hundreds of times before, but I should've been more aware of the dangers." She taps the photo. "Espe-cially as neither of them had any fear."

Like Flo, I think, who moves about the wood like a monkey and never ever looks like she'd fall. I can't take my eyes off that little jar. To think it's all that's left of a once-living person, a person who had a name, a brother, a mother.

"So what did Dad do that made you so angry?" I ask.

With another deep breath, Nell straightens her back.

"Without telling anyone, he took Jacob's ashes. He went quite mad about it," she says. "To this day, he won't tell me where they are."

"Wow!" I say. "What a horrible thing to do!"

No wonder the two of them don't speak anymore. Suddenly I feel sorry for Nell.

"I bet he scattered them in the woods—it makes sense he would've, doesn't it?"

Nell looks rueful. "Yes, my dear, it would make sense. But all he'd say was that the fairies had taken Jacob."

The fairies; I'd guessed as much.

"How do you make sense of *that*?" she asks.

I can't. I don't trust myself to say anything helpful. I could tell her Dad says there's magic in the woods and he thinks I've got a gift for seeing it. She'd tut and roll her eyes, so I could explain that I *have* seen things: green things, golden things like specks of light that I think are fairies. And she'd laugh at me, and I'd understand why. In our family, everyone says Mum's the dreamer while Dad and I are the practical ones. Suddenly it's like everyone's changed places.

"Why did Dad do it?" I ask, because people don't just take another person's ashes. There had to be a reason.

"Ask your father," Nell says. "I'd be fascinated to hear how he justifies himself. Especially now."

I don't know what she means. I can't ask Dad either because he's on his way to London.

"Can't you just tell me?" I ask.

"And let him off the hook?" said Nell. "Absolutely not."

Darkling Cottage
Tuesday, 19 November 1918

Dearest Alfred,

Today Mama received a letter. It said a boy fitting your description was in a hospital in northern France. He is "badly injured" with a wound to the head. More importantly, is he you?

It's left me very shaken, and because of it Mama and Papa have had the biggest row. He even called her "Florrie" instead of "Florence," which he knows she hates. And Anna and Mrs. Cotter are casting doubts over everything—not just about you but my photograph too. It's as if we're all pulling against each other, and I don't like it at all.

Please don't think me ungrateful: "injured" is ten times better than "missing." But I keep picturing the men here in Bexton, with their limps and scars and missing fingers. There's one or two who have burns to the face and wear those ghastly tin masks. Then there are men like Papa whose injuries you can't see. Please say you're not like this.

Mama's completely certain the boy in France is you. She called us all to the drawing room and read his description from the letter—blond hair, green eyes, old scar behind left ear—and I admit it does sound like you. Because of his injuries, the boy doesn't recall his name, but—and this part made my legs go weak—he keeps repeating the word "Bexton."

179

I so wanted it to be you. But also I didn't. Not if you couldn't remember who you were. I want you back just the same as when you went away. Sorry if that sounds awfully selfish.

Mrs. Cotter pointed out that Bexton might be a surname or a house, and Anna agreed, saying that she knew of a town up north with that name. I was almost relieved. Then I grew frightened because it felt as if we'd just found you only for you to slip away from us again. Mama thanked them both for their expert advice, and asked Papa for his view.

All this time he'd been sitting in his chair. I now saw why; his hands shook so much he'd tucked them deep into his armpits. It made me want to put a blanket around his shoulders.

Mama sank at his feet, begging him to believe that the boy was you. Papa said he didn't know what to think. With so many boys lying injured in France, it wasn't wise to get our hopes up. But we'd bring you home and nurse you here, Mama said. It could easily be sorted out. All she asked was that he should believe.

That word again!

Mama had few hard facts, only hope, of which she was full to the brim. It convinced me, Alfred. And it seemed to soften Papa, who eventually agreed she should go to France. It was the only way we'd know if the boy was you. But again he warned her not to get her hopes up. In a very cool tone she said that when she brought you home, then he'd thank her for being hopeful. It struck me as a bit rich because she'd not believed in me and my picture, when clearly Sir Arthur Conan Doyle did!

And, feeling brave, I said so.

While Mama glared, Mrs. Cotter chipped in helpfully, saying to her way of thinking, fairies were just a myth, like ghosts or dragons. Then Anna said people were getting very clever with cameras nowadays, and most pictures like mine were just trickery.

Trickery! Pah! How I wanted to pinch her!

Mama cleared her throat. Slowly, coolly she said I needed to realize it wasn't normal to believe in fairies. At this Papa EXPLODED! I've never heard him rant so—about the war and young men dying for a cause they didn't understand, let alone believe in, and how those who did come home were forgotten because nobody cared. Was it so mad, then, to believe in something good, to hope our sorry, awful world wasn't all there was? Did normal even exist anymore?

Mrs. Cotter and Anna took their cue to leave the room. As Papa went on, I began to grasp it properly. For years we've lived and breathed this dreadful war. The fairies are proof that a better, kinder world still exists. If we believe hard enough, then anything is possible—missing soldiers coming home, ghosts, fairies. By the time Papa had finished, I think even Mama understood: we have to keep our hopes alive if we can.

I left the room unnoticed and went straight to the woods, hoping for fairies. There were rustlings aplenty: mostly squirrels and blackbirds, plus the odd cackling jay. But there was no sign of any fairies, nor the sense that they were near. Even Mr. Glossop's dog had stayed away today, so I couldn't blame their absence on him. The wood seemed full of midwinter gloom. Hard to believe that just days ago

I'd felt magic here, yet that feeling now seemed a thousand miles away. Everything was so bleak and chill, as if the fairies were keeping away on purpose.

That thought stayed with me. At dinner, I couldn't eat pudding, and it was lemon curd tart. I think Mrs. Cotter made it especially to say sorry for earlier, but I'd rather she and Anna had believed me in the first place, or at least not made me feel like a cheat.

Mama is to go to France very soon. She's ever hopeful that the injured boy is you. I know it shouldn't but it scares me a little too, Alfred. What if these things turn out not to be the truth we want? What do we hope for then?

I'm sorry. This would all be so much simpler if you were here.

Do hurry home, Yours ever . . .

29

Wednesday, 20 November

All evening there's no news from the hospital. Just before bed-time, I call Mum, but her phone's switched off, and I've not memorized Dad's number. I try Cheetah Ward too, but it goes straight to the answer phone. Eventually Nell and I go to bed, though it's impossible to sleep.

By two o'clock in the morning, I've given up completely, and I sit by the window with the curtains pulled back. It's a beautiful night. There's a full moon, which makes the sky look almost blue. I open the window and breathe in cold air until my lungs ache. All around the house, trees spread their shadows across the lawn, *for the last time,* I think, because Mr. Giles will be back tomorrow. I feel it like proper pain. We didn't really save the woods today, did we? We just bought ourselves a bit of time.

Then, from the woods comes the sound of an owl. No. Not an owl, because owls don't call like that. Grabbing my jacket and bobble hat, I'm downstairs and out the back door in a flash.

Flo's where she always is. I'm so glad I want to throw my arms right around her, but I can't because she's halfway up the beech tree, ten or more feet higher than the fairy door.

"Hey, Flo! I need to talk to you. Can you come down?"

"Why don't you come up?"

"I'm not getting up there!"

"What are you scared of?"

"Nothing. It's just . . ."

"Just what?"

I'm thinking of Jacob and his fall from a tree—*this* tree, maybe. Hands on hips, I size up the trunk. It looks pretty dangerous to me.

"How safe is it? I mean . . . where do I put my feet?"

Flo laughs. "You've never climbed a tree before?"

"No," I say, irritated. It's hardly a crime. At home there aren't just *trees* all over the place, not like here.

"Look for places to put your feet," Flo says. "Then heave yourself up. Grip with your legs and hands. Once you get to the first big branch you'll be fine."

But I can't see anything to get a hold of.

"Can't you come down?"

Flo sighs. "Will you stop being so flipping sensible for a moment and *try*?"

"I . . . I . . . can't do it."

"You're a child, Alice, not a boring adult," Flo says sternly. "So stop behaving like one."

"That's not fair!" I say.

I'm getting a bit tired of being bossed about by Flo. *Believe in fairies, Alice, talk about your dad, Alice.* Yet I can't remember the last time I did something just for the fun of it.

I stare at the trunk again. Maybe I do want to climb it, after all. I mean, it couldn't hurt. I pull my hat down firmly over my ears.

"Get ready, Flo. I'm coming up."

On the side of the tree is a strong-looking knot in the bark. With my foot resting on it, I reach up to the first branch. It's harder than it looks. The moonlight helps but it throws shadows too. I'm not always certain what's solid and what's thin air. Somehow I haul myself up. My arm muscles burn. Then finally I'm lying across the branch.

The next bit's easier. The branches are closer together, which means I can reach up and push down at the same time. It kills my arms still. But at least I'm moving.

"Well done!" Flo says. "You're getting the hang of it now."

I can't help grinning. It feels good up here, especially if I don't look down.

"Keep going!" she says.

As I reach up, a pigeon bursts from the branch above. Its wings flap about my head.

"Arrgghh!"

I try to shield myself, but I need both hands to hold on. My foot slips and I slam against the trunk. Flo laughs her head off.

"It's not funny!"

"Oh, Alice, you should see yourself!" she says.

I wait for my heartbeat to slow down. Gripping tightly, I heave myself up. The branch creaks; it holds me, though. I ease myself into a crouch, then a standing position. The next branch is nearer. I get onto it like I'm climbing a gate. Flo's boots are just above me now.

One last push.

As I reach up, Flo leans down and grabs a handful of my coat. Now it's easy. Swinging around, I land with a bump beside her.

"Fancy seeing you here," Flo says, grinning.

Pushing the hair off my face, I grin back. "Nice place you've got."

Once I've wedged myself against the branch, it feels safer. If I don't look down, I'll be fine.

"Darkling Wood lives to see another day," I say, though I'm not entirely sure who's behind it all. I'm more worried about what'll happen in the morning.

"Yes, I saw," says Flo.

"Where were you? I thought you'd be with the Travelers."

"No," she says. "I was here in the woods. Tell me, who was that man in the blue jacket?"

"My dad."

"*Your father?* I thought he never . . ."

"He came yesterday evening to take me back to his house, then his car broke down. And you'll never guess, but I found out he had a brother called Jacob who died and . . ."

Flo's eyes go like saucers.

"What?" I ask.

She shakes her head. "Keep going."

"Well, turns out he stole his brother's ashes and . . ." I stop. Flo's still staring at me. "What *is* it? Why are you looking at me like that?"

"It's working," she says. "The fairies' tricks really are working—in ways I'd never thought possible. How incredibly clever they are!"

The thought had crossed my mind too.

"Don't you see, Alice? Your father's car wouldn't start,

186

which just so happened to keep him at his mother's house, the person he's not spoken to for years. It meant they were forced to talk. . . ."

"Shout, more like," I butt in.

"At least you now know why they fell out all those years ago."

"I know Nell's side of things," I correct her. "Not Dad's."

But Flo rubs her hands together like she's really excited. "The fairies' magic has got stronger, don't you see? Strong enough to stop the work taking place today!"

"Yes, but Mr. Giles is coming back in the morning," I say, my sense of dread rising. "I never thought I'd be this super-stitious, Flo, but my brother's got really very ill and if this is the fairies' doing then what the heck's going to happen when the trees come down?"

Flo's hands go still.

"Do you believe in fairies now?" she says.

"I . . . I think so."

She shakes her head. "That's not enough. For their magic to be at its strongest, you need to be absolutely sure."

"You said if I believed I'd see the fairies, and these past couple of days I think I've seen . . ."

"Think?" Flo says. "Alice, you have to *know.*"

I take my hat off and scratch my head. It's easy for Flo to give out orders. She's not got a brother in hospital, or parents who barely speak to each other. She's not miles from her real home.

I look down at my hat, my lovely green bobble hat. Some-thing makes me turn it inside out. Putting it back on, I shift my bum along the branch.

Flo looks at me. "Where are you going?"

"I'm climbing down. I want to try something."

"Be careful!" she calls, but I'm already feeling for the branch below. And the one below that. I keep going until I reach the funny O-shaped branch that's the fairy door.

Lowering myself onto it, I sit, feet dangling down. My heart is thumping fast. I can't see much through the fairy door—just dead leaves and undergrowth.

So I wait. I keep looking, shifting position to get comfortable. Then.

Down on the ground, something moves. I sit forward. It's too dark to see properly . . . and yet *Isn't that a leg? An arm? It can't be—they're tiny!* Sure enough, small, people-shaped shadows begin flitting between the bushes.

"Oh, Flo!" I gasp.

I'm looking straight through the fairy door. And it's a wonder I don't fall out of the tree.

30

They're everywhere: on the ground, in the bushes, on the lower branches of the tree. From the undergrowth more keep coming. Their colors blur together, not just the greens I'd imagined but a big, glowing trail of purples, pinks, and pale blues. And when, for just a second, they do slow down, I see how each one looks different. They've got wings, but they're not birds. They're not insects either, though they move like butterflies. I've never seen anything like them. I must be dreaming. Yet when I rub my eyes and look again, they're still there.

Flo's beside me now, whispering in my ear, "Goodness! They're putting on quite a show for you tonight, Alice."

I don't speak; I'm not sure I can.

Finally, when it seems every bit of woodland is covered with tiny, wing-beating bodies, the creatures settle. As we gaze at them, I know they're watching us too.

"What are they *doing*?" I ask.

"I don't know. They've never behaved like this before."

"That's not good," I say nervously.

"Don't worry, we'll sing to them," Flo says. "They're supposed to like it."

"Not my singing they won't."

We settle on a Christmas carol because it's the only song we both know all the words to. The fairies react like it's a signal. They join hands, reaching up into the bushes, down onto the ground, until every single fairy is connected to another like a long, twisty chain of paper dolls.

Something stirs inside me, forcing me to keep looking, though I can't trust my eyes. The fairies are dancing now. They weave in and out of the trees. It's like watching a trail of moving Christmas lights. *Fairy lights.* An image of Theo flashes into my head. Not how I last saw him, but how I remember him best, his face lit up with happiness. What I'd give for him to see this.

Our singing speeds up. The fairies spin around us in a blur of color. On and on they go, whirling and twisting till it makes me dizzy. I shut my eyes. Now I really can't watch anymore.

Suddenly I sway backward. My arms fly out, but there's nothing to grab hold of. I feel lightness. Then terror. I'm going to fall. At the very last second, Flo seizes my coat.

"Steady there," she says, and somehow I'm sitting squarely on the branch again. It takes me a moment to catch my breath.

When I glance through the fairy door, everything's normal again. The fairies have gone. The bushes and the grass look gray in the moonlight. Not far off an owl shrieks, a proper owl this time. I feel like I've just woken up.

"Did that really happen?" I ask Flo.

"It did," she says. "I've never seen so many before, not all at once like that. And the colors! The fairies I've seen have always worn only green."

We both go quiet. It's almost too much to put into words, like everything I know has just been shaken hard and hasn't fallen back into place. Gradually, though, my head begins to clear. I'm left feeling stiff and cold.

"I'd like to get down," I say to Flo.

Back on solid ground, my legs are like rubber. Flo lands lightly beside me.

"You most definitely believe in fairies now, don't you?" she says.

"I do."

I'm not entirely sure *what* I've just seen. Or how to explain it. When I glance at Flo, she looks a bit shaken too.

"Well, if seeing is believing, then you've given their magic the most astonishing strength!" she says, staring at me in amazement.

"Stop looking at me like that!" I say, but it's sort of nice and makes me glow inside.

"Alice," she says. "Fairies only appear to special people. It's linked to the day and hour of your birth."

I smile. "My dad told me that myth. He says I'm a Chime Child, which means I can see fairies—and ghosts, apparently, though I haven't."

"I hope you believed him. You *are* a special person, you know," says Flo.

My smile gets bigger. Perhaps that's what Dad meant when he told me. I hope he's there at the hospital now, telling Theo he's special too, because it really helps to hear it. Yet as I take in Flo's china-doll face, with its too-big, too-blue eyes, I think *she's* the one who's special.

"Do you live with the Travelers, Flo?"

She tilts her head. It's not a yes or a no.

"I don't know anything about you," I say.

"You saw the fairies because you were ready," she says, not answering me. "Maybe in the morning you'll see other things too."

She sounds so calm, yet I'm still dreading what'll happen when Mr. Giles comes back. I wrap my arms around myself to stop me shivering. We can't lose the wood now.

"Alice, trust me," Flo says. "You must go to school like normal. You'll get into trouble if you don't."

And I'll be in trouble if I do, I think, remembering the history homework I've still not done.

"Don't you have school too?" I ask Flo.

She doesn't reply. Instead she turns and walks off through the trees. I half think about following her, but I don't know where she's heading because, once again, I didn't press her when I asked where she lives.

-{{{{{<

On my way up to bed, I stop to listen for sounds from Nell's room. Everything's quiet. The door behind the curtain must be shut because there's no light coming in; the passage is pitch-black.

All is as it should be.

Except it isn't. I've seen something extraordinary tonight and my brain is still buzzing. I can't go to bed, not yet.

I tiptoe along the passage. Down two steps and I lift the red curtain to one side. Behind the door, the room's lit by moonlight. It makes the keyhole easy to spot. The door is locked; I don't have a key. Searching my coat pockets, I think how in books people use hairpins to open doors like these. All I've got is the pen Max lent me at school.

At the first try, the pen makes a splitting sound. I must have broken it, because the ink part is sticking out, but actually this bit is smaller. More bendy. I'm able to poke it right through the keyhole. Amazingly, the lock clicks. I ease the door open.

The first thing I see is a great wall of words. It's actually the boxes with names written on their sides, but in the moonlight they glow white—"Campbell," mostly, but near the bottom of the pile are more labeled "Waterhouse" than I'd noticed before.

Peering under the table, I look for the jar that once had Jacob in it. It's the only thing left of the uncle I never knew. I want to hold it, just for a moment. But the jar isn't here. What catches the light instead is the pretty box of letters. I don't know why, but I'm a bit intrigued. Tucking it under my arm, I close the door behind me.

Once I'm in bed, I open the box, hoping a bit of reading might help me get to sleep. The letters seem to be in date order. They go from mid to late November 1918.

1918. The end of the war.

I sit up, more alert now. Some letters are in envelopes, some aren't. They're addressed to a person called Alfred Waterhouse at an army base in France. They seem to be written by his sister in Darkling Cottage, and Bexton gets mentioned too. She describes a library, an attic room with awful wallpaper, a warm and cozy kitchen with a door that leads out to the garden.

It's this house.

There's mention of stubborn people—people set in their

ways. How being practical and sensible isn't always the best way to be. And how sometimes it might take something big and awful to convince people that the impossible *can* happen. Most of all, though, there's mention of fairies. It's a sad story. Yet as I read on, a warmth spreads through me, which I think might be hope.

Darkling Cottage
Wednesday, 20 November 1918

To my dearest Alfred,

If that boy in France really is you, then I fear we've much in common because I too am in bed with a wound to my head. Dr. Wyatt had to be dragged from his afternoon tea to tend to me. He brought the good news that Maisie is recovering from her 'flu, but on seeing my dog bites, that cheer disappeared, and much bandaging and aspirin-taking followed. I pity you, Alfred, if you face this every day. It wasn't the slightest bit fun.

Nor, as it turned out, was posting your latest letter earlier today. News of our fairies had reached the village and, in true Bexton style, had been twisted rather out of shape. It started with two boys following me along Glover Street and past the church. Then one of them laughed and I turned around to see them both pulling faces at me, the little brats.

As I joined the post office queue, a ripple went through it. You'd have thought I'd grown a pair of donkey's ears by the way people looked at me! But these were grown-ups and they weren't laughing. In fact, they seemed frightfully sour. Someone mentioned Sir Arthur by name, then another per-

son said anyone with sense would simply let the fairy folk be; their magic was too powerful to be dallied with.

Now I knew the fairies weren't happy—we'd been bombarded with stones and glared at, remember?—so this talk made me very uneasy. Without staying to post your letter, I marched home to get the camera. If Sir Arthur wanted more photos, he could have them, I decided. And that would be the end of it and we could leave the fairies in peace.

Coming down the stairs, I met Mama. She started questioning me about what I was up to and why I looked so pale. I just wanted to get the job done, Alfred. I didn't want a scene. Yet though I made every effort to hide Papa's camera behind my back, she saw it. And as I dodged past her, she called to Papa that I'd taken his camera without asking, and he must go after me IMMEDIATELY.

Once I'd reached our tree, I set up the camera. With Papa in hot pursuit, I didn't have long. Just one more picture was all I wanted. After that I'd leave the fairies well alone.

At first nothing happened. Then, as I kept my eyes on the fairy door, two fairies appeared. One was the color of buttercups, the other the palest green. In the gloom under the trees, they glowed like the prettiest paper lanterns you ever saw. There were no weapons today, no scary grimaces. Instead, their little wings hung limp at their sides and their dear, tiny faces were quite wet with tears. Oh Alfred, I felt awful. My heart was in pieces. I didn't want to be out there in the woods anymore. It was as if my camera and I were trespassing on something very private. It wasn't right at all.

The thing is, someone really was trespassing. Not far off, I heard Mr. Glossop calling to his dog. Instinctively I grabbed the camera. The dog came crashing through the trees toward me. One minute I was upright. The next, I was in the air. The camera flew out of my grasp, and I hit the ground with a thump. Somewhere nearby came another softer thud, then the tinkling of broken glass plates.

Before I could get up, the dog was on me. His teeth snapped at my hair. I kicked. I punched. It made him madder. Something tore at my scalp. The side of my head became warm and wet. My ears started ringing. Then I heard a man shouting. It sounded like Papa. A rifle cracked. Once. Twice. I don't remember anything more.

It's evening as I write to you. I'm tucked up in bed, feeling frightfully sore. I'm sorry if my account sounds dramatic. I don't want to worry you, but I have got quite a wound. There was talk of cutting my hair to get to it, but in the end, Dr. Wyatt managed to stitch my head up all right. The dog had bitten my leg too. That didn't need stitches, but it did need cleaning. And let me tell you, Alfred, that brought tears to my eyes. For your sake, I hope they don't have dogs in France.

Once it was over, I tried to sleep, but my mind wouldn't shut off. I kept thinking of those crying fairies, and how their sadness might somehow be my fault.

It started with the camera, didn't it? Not that I'd meant any harm; I only hoped to prove that fairies did exist. But I suppose that not everyone is meant to see fairies. To be a Chime Child is a special gift, and by taking a picture and then showing it to Papa, and Mama, and the house staff and Sir Arthur, well, I'd not respected that gift, had I? Seeing fairies had suddenly become a not so special thing, and that's why they'd got angry with me.

The realization was a bit much; I did sob rather. Mama

was very nice and sat with me, which made me feel more dreadful about our fight on the stairs. Then she said she had something else to tell me, and I needed to be brave. Papa had been on his way to the woods when he'd heard me screaming. He ran as fast as he could and seized Mr. Glossop's rifle, with which he shot the dog dead. Papa then carried me home. Mama found us in a heap on the back doorstep, both covered in my blood.

After Dr. Wyatt had seen to me, she said, he'd tended to Papa. Only Papa's head couldn't be put back together with stitches. He's still not recovered from his time at the Front, and after firing that gun today, he took a turn for the worse.

So it was decided he should go away for a while to a special place to rest.

And so now I don't know what to think, Alfred. Those fairies brought Papa and me such hope. So too did the letter from France. But who knows the truth of it really?

My head hurts terribly, so I'll leave it there.

Until tomorrow,
Your sister

31

Wednesday, 20 November
(morning)

Dad phones first thing to say Theo is stable. "A small step," he calls it, but it feels such a massive relief. So I go to school like Flo says, because it beats waiting for Mr. Giles to arrive. First lesson, Max greets me with a bigger than usual smile.

"You're here!" he says. "So the news from the hospital is good, right?"

I nod. Relief flashes across his face. It makes my nose tingle like I'm about to cry, but then his smile comes back and it makes me smile too.

"Hi, Alice," says Ella. "Everything okay?" She means Theo, of course.

"Yes, Theo's a bit better this morning, thanks."

"I'm glad to hear that," she says. "Now, is it okay for me to sit with you two or am I going to feel like a gooseberry?"

Max laughs, but I blush to my hair roots. Then, as Ella sits next to me, I see she's still wearing her "Save Darkling Wood" badge. She notices me looking at it.

"Don't worry," she says, serious now. "We won't block the

lane while your dad needs to get to the hospital. But we will be back, you know."

My stomach flutters, though this time not for Max.

"I know. It isn't over yet."

After lunch, it's history. Before the lesson even starts, Mrs. Copeland comes over and crouches down by my desk so her face is level with mine.

"Good to see you, Alice," she says. "We're doing more of the project talks today, but if you're not ready to do yours—and I know you had a chat with Mr. Jennings about homework—it's fine. You've had a tough few days."

The letters are here with me in a carrier bag. All day I've had the handle hooked over my arm because I mustn't lose them, though I don't think Nell's noticed they've gone.

Behind me, someone mutters, "Detention." I take a big breath. "I am ready, miss."

But she's on her feet again, glaring at the back row.

"Stop that!" she says firmly.

Turning around, Ella joins in. "Yeah, shut up, you lot! Alice's got a flipping good reason for missing her homework, so don't start on her, all right?"

The class goes very quiet.

"Thank you, Ella," says Mrs. Copeland. She looks daggers at the back row boys. "Any more stupid, ignorant remarks and you'll go straight to Mr. Jennings, do you hear me?"

No one speaks.

"Good. Now, Max, would you do your talk first, please?"

He strolls up to the front and does a little bow. A few people whoop. Mrs. Copeland glares; the class settles down again.

On the screen at the front, Max shows us an old sepia

photo. It's of a very young-looking man in an army uniform that's clearly too big for him because he's had to roll up his sleeves.

"This is my great-great-grandfather George Giles," says Max proudly. "The war was over before he was old enough to join up, so he joined the medical corps.

"When all the injured soldiers came home, he trained to be a nurse."

It's hard to imagine so many young people sick or dying. And yet there's George grinning at the camera. Amazing. I think of Theo's nurse, Jo, who stayed so calm and cheerful, and of Mum trying to be positive. It seems to help get people through.

There's clapping when he finishes. Max sits down again, catching my eye as he does.

"Well done!" I whisper.

He smiles. It's a lovely smile.

"You two, honestly!" Ella groans.

Next a girl talks about war medals. Afterward, her friend goes up to talk about the Spanish Flu epidemic, which killed even more people than the war. It goes on like this—more students taking their turn—until I think Mrs. Copeland's forgotten me.

I put my hand up. "I haven't had a go yet, miss."

"Then come on, Alice," she says.

Getting out of my seat, I walk to the front. Mrs. Copeland claps for quiet. By now, though, the class is getting bored. Two girls are drawing on a pencil case. A boy at the back has already put his coat on: Mrs. Copeland swiftly tells him to take it off.

She nods to me. "Ready?"

It's dead silent. My throat goes tight. Did I really think I could stand up here and talk about fairies? *I* might believe in them, but still.

I look at Mrs. Copeland. I'm stuck.

"What's in the bag?" she says helpfully.

The carrier bag's still wrapped around my wrist. It takes agonizing seconds to get it off. Once I have, I shake the letters out onto the table and put them into date order.

"Are they love letters?" asks a girl sitting next to Ella.

A giggle ripples around the class. I try not to go red.

"No," I say. "They're from a girl to her brother who's coming home from the war."

Mrs. Copeland leans forward. "Original letters? How interesting! Where did you get them?"

"I found them in my grandmother's house. . . ." I hesitate. Thirty faces stare back at me.

"What does she write about?" Mrs. Copeland asks.

"How she misses her brother, what it's like to be a girl in 1918, how her mother expects her to be more ladylike."

A boy in the front row starts doodling on his book. Mrs. Copeland clicks her fingers. Reluctantly he puts down his pen.

Then a hand goes up. It's Max. "What about her dad? Did he fight in the war too?"

"He did, though he was injured. He got into photography as a hobby, and one day someone really famous came to talk to him about his pictures."

Now the class are interested.

"Who was it?" Max asks.

"Sir Arthur Conan Doyle."

Mrs. Copeland's mouth drops open. "Gosh!" she says. "He wrote the Sherlock Holmes series. He was very interested in photography. In fact, he believed that it was possible to photograph fairies. It was a huge story at the time."

I nod.

"Two girls took some pictures of what they claimed were fairies. Some people thought they were fakes, but a lot believed they were real."

"Oh," I say, shuffling the letters. "I didn't know that."

Mrs. Copeland goes to her computer and types something in. Seconds later a black-and-white picture flashes up on the projector screen.

"This photograph's the most famous one," she says. The class immediately starts talking about it.

"That's not real!" someone says.

"They're made of paper, anyone can see that!" says a boy at the back.

The photograph shows the head and shoulders of a girl about my age. Chin resting on her hand, she's gazing at a group of little people. They're right in front of her on a leaf or something, holding hands as they dance in a ring.

It's a stupid picture. The so-called fairies are obviously paper cutouts. Even the girl is looking past them, not *at* them. It's like the whole thing's been botched together for a joke. Perhaps the pictures taken in Darkling Wood were like this. Maybe my letter-writer played a prank on the world, and we've all been taken in.

I don't believe it, though. Not after what I saw last night.

Max puts his hand up again. "I don't get it, miss. If he invented Sherlock Holmes, who's a genius, why did Arthur Conan Doyle think this picture was real? I mean, he wasn't exactly an idiot, was he?"

"It wasn't just him. Thousands of other people believed it too," Mrs. Copeland says. "Any idea why?"

Hands go up.

"Because he'd make money," Ella says.

"He was rich enough already," Mrs. Copeland says.

"Because he was weird," says someone else. The class laughs. Mrs. Copeland pulls a face.

"Think about it," she says. "Why would people believe in fairies, especially just after the war?"

The girl in the letters said fairies brought her hope. Just like Max's great-great-granddad smiling for all those injured soldiers. Just like me hoping Theo will get well again and Dad and Nell will make peace. And just like Flo leaving daft notes up trees. It might not be real, but it gets us through.

Before I know it, my hand's in the air.

"Yes, Alice?"

"Did Arthur Conan Doyle lose anyone in the war, miss?"

"Yes, he lost his son and other relatives too. Many people did."

"So maybe, with so much horrible stuff going on, well, perhaps no one knew what was real anymore. And it made them feel better if they could hope for something different and better. It made them less miserable."

Everyone looks at me like I've just spoken French. But Mrs. Copeland nods enthusiastically. "Yes, that's a really good point."

Then Max says, "What happens in the end, Alice? Does her brother come home?"

"I don't know. It doesn't say."

Another class, already dismissed, charges past our window.

People start putting their books away, and Mrs. Copeland asks us to tuck our chairs in as we leave. Max is the only person still listening.

"Why did you do your talk on fairies?" Max asks, once everyone else has gone.

I hold up the carrier bag. "Actually, it was about these letters."

"Which happen to be about fairies."

"So?"

"My dad's gone back to cut down your grandmother's wood today and you come to school full of fairies."

I'm not sure what he's getting at. I wish he hadn't mentioned the wood either. Despite what Flo said last night, I'm still scared the fairies' magic won't be strong enough to stop Mr. Giles today.

"You know the stories about Darkling Wood, don't you?" Max says. "About how certain trees there are magical?"

I shoot him a look. "What if they're not stories?"

"Aren't they?"

I look at him again, properly this time. His eyes are brown with gold flecks in them. They're not reason enough to trust him. But he's the son of a tree surgeon so maybe he does know stuff: I decide to tell him.

As we walk to the shed where Max's bike is locked up, I talk about last night. What I saw in the woods. How it felt. He's wide-eyed and silent. I'm not quite sure what I expect him to *do* exactly, but he listens carefully.

By the time I've finished, I've completely missed my bus and have to catch the public one out on the main road. As the bus pulls away, I'm feeling nervous again—about the woods, about Theo, about everything, really.

We drive past Max, who's on the pavement, bike against his hip, talking into his phone. I wonder who he's speaking to because he looks so serious. Probably just a friend.

Yet a nasty voice in my head says I should've kept quiet. Telling people about fairies didn't help the girl in the letters. Maybe Max is already spreading it around, and he couldn't even wait till he got home.

32

The bus drops me in the village. From here, it takes just under fifteen minutes to reach Darkling Wood on foot. I can't decide if I want to rush home to see what's happened or to walk extra slowly. Either way, I'm sick with nerves.

I'm halfway up the hill when Mr. Giles's jeep comes tearing down it. He's driving so fast it almost knocks me into the hedge.

"Road hog!" I shout after him.

He must've come from Nell's, I realize, and it makes my stomach leap. I can't bear not knowing any longer. I have to see what he's done—or not done—to the trees. I start running. I don't stop till I've reached Darkling Wood.

At first glance, nothing's changed. I gasp with relief. The trees are still here, pressing tall and dark around the house. Something's been cut, though, because there's sawdust on the grass like a sprinkling of snow.

Then I see it.

It's happened to the two trees nearest the house. Right

near the top on each one there are gaps where branches used to be. It's clear as anything—the cut bark stands out orange against the trunk. On the ground underneath, the branches lie in a mangled heap.

A new whoosh of sickness comes over me. The magic wasn't strong enough after all. Mr. Giles came here today and started work. Despite everything, we couldn't save Darkling Wood.

"The tree surgeon chap's just been called away."

I spin around to see Dad coming toward me across the lawn. He looks tired. Pale. He really needs a shave.

"How's Theo?" I ask, heart in mouth. "Is he any better?"

"He is," says Dad.

"Better than when we spoke this morning?"

"I think so. They've upped his medication. It seems to be working."

I breathe normally again. This is *very* good news.

"Poor Mr. Giles, though—his son has just had an accident," says Dad. "He fell off his bike, apparently."

The sick feeling lands back in my stomach.

"Max? But I only saw him half an hour ago!"

"Don't look so upset, Alice," Dad says. "It didn't sound life-threatening."

I forget all about Max being on his phone now. I'm worried. If he rides a bike like his father drives a van, it's bound to be bad.

"I'll ask Nell if I can call Mr. Giles," I say, turning for the house.

Dad stops me with a hand on my arm. "I'm sure it's not serious. Let Mr. Giles get home to his son first."

"He's called Max," I say.

Dad smiles. "Is he a friend from school?" I nod. "Then you'd better call this *Max* tonight, if you can last that long."

My face goes hot at Dad's teasing. But he's quickly serious again.

"Walk with me for a bit?" he says.

"All right."

Sidestepping the cut-down branches, we enter the wood. Soon the pile of branches will be bigger. There'll be more lop-sided trees. More orange scars.

Or will there?

Not if Mr. Giles gets called away again. Not if Dad's here long enough to talk to Nell. I don't want Max to be hurt, and yet I feel a flicker of hope. Theo's getting better. The woods aren't gone yet. I think the fairies' magic is still working.

Only maybe now they need a little help.

I stare at Dad's back, up ahead on the path. It's now or never. I grit my teeth.

"Nell told me what you did," I say.

Dad turns his head slightly; he's listening.

"Taking your brother's ashes was a rubbish thing to do, Dad."

He clears his throat.

"You must've had a reason. What did Nell do to you?"

He stops. Turns to look at me. "What are you talking about, Alice? Who says she *did* anything?"

"She does."

"Then ask her. I'm sure she'll be happy to fill you in."

"She says I should hear it from you."

Dad rolls his eyes. "Drop it, will you?"

"Nell says that would be letting you off the hook." He

laughs, but not in a funny way. Then he looks skyward. At the ground. Anywhere rather than at me.

"I can't talk about it. Not now this has happened with Theo."

I miss a breath.

"*Theo?* What the heck does you stealing your brother's ashes have to do with him?"

"Leave it, Alice."

Dad starts walking again, faster now, hands stuffed in his pockets. I go after him. I'm not *leaving* anything. No way.

"If this is about Theo, then I've a right to know!" I say.

No answer.

"Dad! You can't just bring Theo up, then leave it dangling. That's really not fair!"

Dad charges on ahead through branches and brambles that flick back into my face. The path takes a sharp left. There are trees on either side of us. Big, strong, towering trees. And I know I should be glad they're still here, that Mr. Giles hasn't got this far, but all I can think of is what Dad's just said.

We end up at the beech tree. I'm not exactly surprised. This is Flo's special tree, and after last night I suppose it's mine. Only it won't be anyone's special tree for much longer, not unless we finish this.

Dad rests his hand on the trunk.

"Jacob died falling from this tree," he says.

Jacob: he's a real person to me now, that funny boy in the striped jumper, hanging upside down from a branch.

"I guessed that," I say, though I don't mention I've climbed the tree too—and against Nell's wishes.

"He was only eleven. I was older. Old enough to know better."

209

"Nell doesn't blame you for the accident, Dad." Dad's hand falls to his side. He does another of his not-funny laughs.

"No, but she never felt the same about this place afterwards. And she does blame me for taking his ashes."

"Well, you *did* take his ashes."

"Do you know what *she* took?" he says, flaring up. "Well? *Do* you?"

"No." I take a step back. "That's why I asked."

I'm sensing it's got something to do with fairies.

33

Dad's crying now in big hard sobs.

"She took his heart, Alice. He was eleven years old and she took his heart."

I stare at him. I don't understand.

"He belonged in these woods. This was where his heart was." He stamps the ground with his foot. "Right here."

I nod. I think I follow that part.

"But Nell had other plans. He was a healthy young boy, so she made him a . . ." He pauses. Clears his throat: ". . . a donor. His heart was given to someone else."

I nod again. I want him to keep talking, though I try to hide my shock. I mean, Jacob? A heart donor? This is a massive thing to take in.

"But that's good, surely," I say, thinking of how long we waited for a match, with Theo getting sicker every day. Then I look into Dad's face. *"Isn't it?"*

"It should've been. Except the person who got Jacob's heart rejected it and died anyway, a week after surgery."

I go cold.

"Oh," I say. "That's . . ."

"Awful. Sad. Painful," Dad cuts in. "Yes, it was. That poor family's hopes were raised and then dashed again within a matter of days."

It feels uncomfortably close. Too close. Dad and I both fall silent. All around us the woods are quiet too, but what's charging around my head feels deafening.

Dad's the first to speak again.

"I was never happy with Nell's idea from the start. I just couldn't . . . you know . . . handle the thought of Jacob's heart still alive inside someone else. I couldn't bear it that part of him was out there in the world and he wasn't here with us."

I know what Dad means. When I saw Theo, it was strange to think of another person's heart pumping away inside him. How that person was loved and missed just as much as we loved Theo. And how part of that person still survived.

"It's not a bad thing Nell did," I say. "Where would Theo be now without a donor? At least someone gets to live."

"But not Jacob," Dad says through clenched teeth.

I don't know what to say. In my head, though, things are getting clearer. This is why Dad got so scared, isn't it? Why he stopped seeing us when Theo got really sick. Why he punched a wall at the hospital that day and why his hands shook all the way home in the car. It doesn't excuse it, but it is starting to make sense.

Dad takes a deep breath and rolls his shoulders. "So now you know," he says, as if that's finished and we can all move on.

I'm not ready. There's something else.

"All this time we've had to manage without you, Dad," I say. "You should have stuck with us, not gone off to Devon. We'd have been all right."

212

Dad sighs. Pulls a face. Something in me snaps.

"Don't look like that!" I cry. "We're your family! You can't just replace us with another one—a *better* one—because you got bored of us!"

"Alice, come on . . ." He opens his arms.

I step back. "Well, I hope you're happy! Because actually we've got along JUST FINE without you!"

I'm shaking with anger. Dad messed it up with us and here he is, still messing up with Nell. It's pathetic.

"You'd better tell Nell what you did with those ashes!" I say. "You can't just walk away from her too!"

Dad won't look at me.

"Especially if they are here in the woods. Before she cuts the lot down. Before it's too late."

"Why?"

Is he that dumb? Do I really have to spell it out?

"Because, *Dad,* this is your big chance to do something right for a—"

"Alice! Alice! Are you there?"

It's Nell. I see her blue jumper through the trees. She's coming our way. I stare at Dad.

"Now's your chance," I say.

Borage finds us first. He puts his paws on my shoulders and lands a big doggy lick on my nose.

"There you are," says Nell, stepping into the clearing.

"I was just coming to ask . . . Oh." Seeing Dad, she stops dead.

Gently, I push Borage off because I need to breathe.

"Dad and I have been talking," I say.

Dad fidgets with his car keys like he's planning his escape.

"Really?" says Nell drily.

"And we agree"—I glare at Dad—"*don't we*, that it's time this thing between you got sorted."

Neither of them speaks. It goes on like that for a good few minutes: two grown people staring at their feet like they're kids in the playground at school. Then Dad tips his head back and looks up into the beech tree. For a second, I think he's seen Flo. Then he moves closer to the trunk, reaches up on tiptoe, and puts his hand into the fairy door. He pulls out a piece of paper. It's that same expensive-looking note Flo and I almost fell out over. I've no idea what Dad's doing with it now.

"You always did like to use my best stationery, David," says Nell as he gives her the note.

Through the thick paper I can just make out the words:

PLEASE KEEP MY BROTHER SAFE.

I look at Nell. The paper trembles in her hands. She tilts her chin toward the fairy door. "Is Jacob here?"

I cover my mouth with both hands. The note isn't about Theo. No wonder Flo didn't understand why I was so upset.

This note is from Dad.

"He was. I left his ashes here," Dad says, indicating the branch where last night Flo and I sat. "The fairies took him away."

"David . . . ," says Nell.

I try to picture what someone's ashes might look like—dust, I suppose, or sand. Certainly nothing like a boy in a striped jumper hanging upside down from that same branch.

Dad keeps talking. "Jacob loved this tree. He always said he could see fairies through the hole. I never saw them myself, but he was adamant he could. He said one day he wanted to join them."

Despite everything, I feel myself smiling inside. It's not exactly a happy ending, but when I think of how beautiful those fairies were, I'm glad Jacob's resting place was here. Yet Nell's working her jaw like mad. She looks ready to explode.

Very carefully, she folds the piece of paper and puts it in her pocket. She takes a deep breath. Then she crouches down at the base of the tree, putting her hands flat on the ground as if she's warming them before a fire. She shuts her eyes. Goes very still. The only thing moving is the tears rolling down her face.

By the time Nell gets to her feet again, the light is already fading. Cool, heavy night air hangs between the trees.

"I don't believe in fairies, David," she says.

"No," Dad says. "You've always been clear on that."

"Just as *you* didn't believe in organ donation." She sounds sharp as ever; I'm not sure anything has changed.

"But," she says, "life has a funny way of working these things out for us. You have had Theo's plight to contend with, and I now have a place to come and think about my son."

"And the woods?" Dad asks.

As Nell looks up at the trees, a smile spreads across her face. "Do you know, I may have been a little overzealous in my plans for the wood—Mr. Giles has been trying to tell me so all day. I'll have a word with him, see if we can't just clear the trees closest to the house."

Then she goes up to Dad until she's only inches away. I hold my breath. Her hand touches him on the shoulder. I'm shocked by how gentle she is.

"My dear," she says. "You did what Jacob would've wanted. It's time I accepted that fact."

Nell and Dad walk back to the house—not arm in arm or anything, but they're talking in normal voices, which is a good start. I let them go on ahead. Borage stays with me, sniffing the air.

The sky has gone very pale, which makes the trees look darker, stronger. The magic of this place makes my skin prickle. And now it's done. It's over. The woods are saved. I keep an eye out for Flo; I've so much to tell her. But it goes on getting darker, and she doesn't come.

"Come on, Borage," I say after a while. "Let's go." We'll come back tomorrow, because I know Darkling Wood will still be here.

34

Thursday, 21 November

When I wake up the next morning, something's different; at first I can't work out what. It's not the dinner we ate together like a family, or Dad staying the night on Nell's sofa, though all that's different enough.

As I sit up and rub my eyes, I see what's changed. The whole room looks brighter. There's even a little line of sunshine coming in under the curtains. I get dressed quickly and head downstairs. In the hallway, there's a big patch of sunlight on the floor where I've never seen it before. And Nell's being unusually polite to someone on the phone.

"Pollarding? So that should slow their growth down, yes? Good. Excellent, Mr. Giles," she says.

Through the open sitting-room door, I see Dad's feet sticking out from under a blanket.

I hover in the doorway. "What's pollarding, Dad?"

"Huh? Pollarding?" He sits up, bleary-eyed. "It's a bit like pruning. You cut something back to stop it growing so fast."

"A trim, then." Though I expect this sounds too much like hairdressing for Nell. Turning to her, I wave to get her attention.

"Ask how Max is!" I hiss. "Can I speak to him?" But she's still in full flow on the phone.

"What you cut yesterday has already improved the light situation here. It's really rather remarkable. The whole house feels different."

Eventually, she asks, "Your son—has he recovered from yesterday's mishap?"

There's a long, nerve-racking wait as Nell ums and ahs to Mr. Giles's reply.

"Well, well," she says finally. "It's as if some malign force was against us all along."

She's nearer the truth than she realizes, but Nell being Nell simply laughs it off. Then, ignoring my outstretched hands, she puts the phone down.

"Was Max too ill to speak?" I ask, feeling awful.

"On the contrary, my dear, he's on his way to school," says Nell.

"Hang on, so it wasn't a bad accident, then?"

"It wasn't an *accident* at all. Max made it up."

"What? Why?"

"According to his father, Max did it for you," Nell says, raising her eyebrows at me. Which makes me blush. Mostly, though, I'm pretty chuffed.

The rest doesn't take much working out. Once I told him about the fairies, Max knew we had to save the woods. So he lied, knowing how his father would stop work at once and rush home.

"I owe Max a thank-you," I say, though maybe even that was the fairies' work and I should be thanking them too.

Halfway through breakfast, the phone rings.

"I'll get it," I say, thinking it might be Mum.

When I pick up the phone, no one speaks. I hear a person breathing.

"Very funny, weirdo."

"I'm not a weirdo," says a voice. I almost drop the phone.

"Theo?"

"Alice?"

My throat goes thick. I do a quick fan of my face to keep back the tears. "You little monkey! I'm calling your doctor immediately! DOCTOR!"

Theo laughs. It's a proper giggle that makes me sunshine-happy. I hear Mum in the background telling him not to get too excited. But we carry on until she takes the phone off him.

"Hi, Alice," she says. "Lexie's mum's had her baby at last and they're out of hospital. Jen's coming with Lexie to pick you up today."

I stop smiling. "What?"

"They'll get to you about lunchtime—well, that's what she said, so let's hope her timekeeping's better than Kate's. The main thing is, you don't have to go with Dad or stay on with Nell, okay?"

I twirl the telephone cord around my finger. I don't actually know if it *is* okay.

"I'm all right here," I say.

Mum sighs. "I thought you'd be happy, Alice." Now the tears start tumbling down my face.

"I am happy," I say. "I really am."

I don't go to school today, which I'm not exactly sad about; I can't say I'll miss Ferndean High. But I am sad not to say goodbye to Ella or Max, so I make sure I ask Nell for Mr. Giles's phone number.

Then there's Flo. I'm halfway out the back door when Nell stops me.

"Pack first," she says. "And clean your room."

I glare at her. She can't be serious, not when I've got so much to tell Flo.

Dad looks up from his bacon sandwich. "Just do it, love."

So I stomp back upstairs, but it's funny, really. No one's ever had to tell me to tidy my room. And now that they have, I'm a tiny bit pleased.

It takes all of two minutes to stuff clothes in a bag and straighten the covers on my bed. I take the letters out of the carrier and return them to their box. I'm careful to put them back as I found them, in date order, tied with green ribbon. Once I've finished, they look untouched. Just as they've always been.

Yet something has very definitely changed. Me, for starters.

Once Borage sees bags in the hallway, he won't leave my side. He insists on coming with me to the woods.

"No frightening Flo, d'you hear?" I say as we go down the path. He twitches his ears to show he's heard.

But I think of a million reasons why she won't be here: school, illness, Travelers moving on—if she's a Traveler at all. I'm so deep in thought I'm not watching where I'm going. I walk straight into something very hard.

"Ahhh!" I clutch my forehead. "What the . . . ?"

"You should look where you're going," laughs Flo. Squinting upward, I see the boots I've just walked into. My head throbs like mad and already there's a lump beneath my fingers. But that doesn't stop the big, happy *whoop* in my chest.

"You're here!"

"Where else would I be?"

Which makes perfect sense, coming from her.

"You won't believe it, but my grandmother's changed her mind! She's not cutting down the wood after all! Isn't it brilliant?"

There's a silence. I wish I could see Flo's face.

"It's more than brilliant, Alice," she says finally. "You did it. You believed in magic."

"I believed in bad magic as well as the good stuff," I say, thinking of Theo on the phone this morning and how different things might've been. "But now I'm going home today, so I'd rather not say goodbye to a pair of boots."

Flo drops down beside me with a thud and I burst out laughing.

"Ow! That hurt!" she says, shaking out her feet.

"What's so funny?"

"You did that the first time I met you—well, the first *proper* time," I say.

As she pushes her hair off her face, I see her nose has gone pink.

"Are you crying?"

"No." But as she dabs her eyes in her coat sleeve, it's obvious she is.

"I'll think of you each time I climb a tree, and whenever I see—"

"You won't," she cuts in.

"Oh?"

"You saw fairies when you needed to. And that's more than most people ever do."

Now it's my turn to fill up. I'm so sad I ache. But it's sad in a good way because something amazing happened, even if it never does again.

"In that case, I'm glad I saw fairies with you, Flo."

"Oh Alice, I'm glad too."

Borage, who has been sniffing around the trees, picks this moment to lollop over. He looks like a giant wolf. Flo breathes in sharply.

"Send him away!" she gasps.

Borage stops, ears down, eyes mournful.

"He's all right. Look at him—he's a softie."

As if to prove it, Borage lies down and rolls over. Flo stares at him, eyes on stalks.

Then, after a bit, she says, "I ... I think ... maybe ... he wants a tummy rub?"

"He *always* wants a tummy rub," I say.

At first, it's just me doing the stroking. But eventually Flo kneels beside me. She touches his front paw. Then his upside-down head. The tip of his tail thumps against the ground. We sit down with Borage stretched out blissfully between us. And we stay like that for ages, until I hear a car.

It's Jen and Lexie. They're early. Grinning, I scramble to my feet.

"Come and meet Lexie!" I say to Flo.

I go on ahead, back to the house. The garden is full of voices I know well, yet it's strange to hear them here at Darkling Cottage. As soon as I'm through the gate, I see Lexie talking to Dad. I've forgotten how much I've missed her.

Once we've hugged and squealed, Lexie takes out her phone and shows me a photo.

"Alice," says Lexie, "meet Baby."

The baby gazes out at us with eyes so blue they look black.

"Adorable," I say. "But *Baby*?"

"We can't agree on a name," Jen calls over. "Got any suggestions, Alice? We're well and truly stuck."

I look at Lexie, blowing kisses to the picture, and smile.

"Brother or sister?" I ask.

"A little sister," Lexie says, not taking her eyes off her phone.

I don't know why, but I'm glad.

The gate clicks open and there's Flo. I think she's been hanging back, waiting for us to stop squealing. As she crosses the lawn toward us now, her long coat trails in the grass.

I touch Lexie's arm. "There's someone I'd like you to say hi to."

She looks up. Flo stops a few feet away. She's so small next to Lexie. So thin.

"Flo, this is my very good friend Lexie from home," I say. "Lexie, this is my very good friend Flo from . . . the woods."

I wait for them to smile and say hello or something. But Flo puts her hands in her pockets and Lexie frowns.

"What's the matter?" I ask.

"Who are you talking to, Alice?" Lexie says.

"Flo. I told you."

"But it's just us. Everyone else has gone inside."

I don't know what she's on about. Flo's right in front of me. So close I can almost touch her hand.

Lexie's mouth falls open. "Blimey, Alice, no wonder you're seeing stuff. You've got a massive bump on your head."

She's right; it feels the size of a golf ball.

"I'm fine," I say.

"I'm fine," laughs Lexie. "You *always* say that. Sometimes it's okay to be *not fine* too, you know."

Within moments, Nell, Dad, Jen, and Borage are all crowding around me. Over their shoulders I watch as Flo slips away between the trees.

35

Today is Theo's birthday. Just like the last time we had a party, we tie balloons to the gate so people can find our house. Only this time, instead of an ambulance, an old car pulls up with a dog on the backseat, and that dog goes nuts when he sees me.

The day's so warm we set up tables and chairs in the garden. Mum's made Theo an amazing cake, which she's covered in black and white icing so it looks like a football. Kate and Jen bring Jell-O and ice cream; we have to eat this first to stop it melting.

Then it's cake time. We watch anxiously as Theo breathes in. I'm sure I'm not the only one remembering this moment on another birthday. Today, though, he blows out all eight candles in one go. It means there's spit on the icing, but no one really minds, least of all Dad, who eats three slices.

The little girl on his knee prefers chewing dinosaurs; Theo's T. rex is her favorite. I'm worried she's going to swallow a plastic paw or something, but when I try to take it off her she shrieks, and Dad frowns like I'm being mean. By the time Theo notices, she's already bitten off the tail.

"Wow, Poppy!" he says. "You took on the T. rex and won!"
She gives him her biggest gummy smile.

"You like Theo, don't you, Pops?" says Dad. "And what about Alice, eh? She's a bossy big sister, isn't she?"

"*Half* sister, Dad," I say.

After cake, Theo wants us all to play football. But it's far too hot and, apart from Lexie, we're useless. So in the end it's just Lexie who keeps playing. She lets Theo tackle her to the ground, and when he scores a goal, he runs around with his arms out airplane-style. We all cheer and whoop like mad.

"It is remarkable, isn't it?" Nell says to me. "He looks so well."

"Theo *is* well. The hospital say he's doing brilliantly now."

"I suppose things have moved on since Jacob's day," she says.

I nod, lump in throat. But she doesn't just mean Theo or Jacob; she's watching Dad, who's got tears dripping onto his shirt.

The whooping and cheering goes on. In seconds, Dad goes from tears to laughter and gets to his feet to referee. All the while, he holds Poppy's hand as she trips alongside him through the grass. I watch Mum watching them and wonder what she's thinking. How it feels for her. When she looks away, she's smiling. Maybe things have moved on there too.

As the game drifts down to the bottom of the garden, Nell nudges me with her elbow.

"Before I forget, here. This came through my letterbox." She slides a birthday card envelope across the table. It's got Theo's name on it in familiar wonky writing.

I grin. The writing belongs to Max. He's been kind about Theo—he's kind about lots of things. We keep in touch by text and often talk online, and when Theo and I go and stay at Darkling Cottage this summer, I'll get to see him all the time.

As if on cue, Borage pushes his wet nose against my hand. Ever hopeful, he stares at what's left of the cake.

I'm itching to give him some, but Nell's frowning like she's got something more to say.

"What is it?" I ask.

"You read Florence's letters," she says. "It's all right. I know."

"Oh. I mean, how?"

"You didn't put them back. I found them in your room, dear," she says. "That last day everything was such a rush."

I look at her. "Did you say *Florence*?"

"I did. The girl who wrote those letters was called Florence."

"But I thought her mum was Florence. Or Florrie. It says so in one of the letters, the one where her parents fall out about that boy in France."

Nell nods. "It was quite common back then for children to be named after their parents and grandparents."

I picture those letters, all tucked away inside that box on the floor of that little room. I'm still not sure why they're there, in Nell's house.

So I ask.

"Aha!" says Nell, one finger raised. Leaning sideways, she reaches into her bag and pulls out a thick blue book. It's another photo album like the one with Jacob's picture in it, only this one looks more expensive. Between us we clear a space for it on the table. She doesn't open it, not straightaway, though she marks a certain page with her finger.

"Before I married your grandfather, my surname was Waterhouse," she says.

So that's why those trunks had "Waterhouse" written on them. *Now* I get it.

"And this is Florence Waterhouse the younger. It's the only picture I could find of her—I thought you'd like to see."

As the album falls open, I think I know what's coming. I feel a strange flutter under my ribs. There are other pictures on the page, other people smiling for the camera. But my eyes go straight to her.

"She was a pretty thing, wasn't she?" says Nell. I nod. She was.

Immediately, I recognize the red coat and the white nightgown-type dress. I always thought how bizarrely she'd dressed. Yet in this old picture, it doesn't look out of place.

"Does that mean Florence was your ..." I do a quick working-out. "Grandmother?"

Nell shakes her head. "Two years after those letters were written, Mrs. Waterhouse and her husband had another child—Edward, my grandfather."

"Oh. Right. So what about ...?"

I stop. It's dawning on me what happened. Nell looks so solemn it can only mean one thing: Flo didn't recover from her dog bites.

Yet the girl in the picture is smiling. It's a huge, lit-up smile that reaches her eyes. Perhaps this was the one taken by her father when she'd just seen fairies. Darkling Wood is there in the background. And she looks so alive it's hard to imagine her being anything else.

"What about the pictures she took of the fairies?" I ask Nell. "Are they in here too?"

"They're not. They didn't survive either. Apparently, Florence destroyed them herself because she was convinced they'd brought the family bad luck. She didn't think the fairies ever forgave her."

Which explains why she was so keen to save the wood and why she knew what might happen if we didn't.

"Did Alfred bring the letters home with him?" I ask hopefully, for I want something in this story to have worked out.

Again Nell shakes her head. "They were 'returned to sender.' Apparently they reached Darkling Cottage before the official telegram."

"So it wasn't him in the hospital in France after all?"

"No, it wasn't. The letters arrived back at Darkling Cottage with 'KILLED' stamped in red on the top envelope," Nell says.

I blink back tears. It's so sad. I can't imagine the poor Waterhouse family getting such horrible news.

"That top envelope wasn't with the others in the box," I say.

"No," Nell says. "My grandfather said no one could bear to look at it, so they threw it on the fire."

Nell puts the album back in her bag and we sit in silence. It's loads to think about. Even today, on such a happy, lovely day, there still seems so much sadness in my family.

"What are you two moping about?" says Mum, appearing at the table. "Come on! It's photograph time!"

Nell and I groan. But I think we're both glad to get up and do something just to break the spell. We're done with talking about the dead.

It's decided I'll take the picture with the new phone Dad bought me. Once everyone's in position, I look at the screen and see Mum and Theo, Dad and Poppy, Jen and Kate and Lexie with baby Nancy nestled in between them. And on the end is Nell, standing straight with Borage at her feet.

"Get on with it, then," says Dad.

"Yes, Alice, don't keep your father waiting," says Mum. "He's not got all the time in the world."

"No need for that, Carrie," Nell chips in.

"I'm just saying, that's all," says Mum. "I expect Lara will be—"

"All right!" Dad snaps back.

Poppy chooses this moment to start howling. Jen and Kate look uncomfortable, and Borage, sensing a mood change, gets up and tries to sniff Nancy's nappy.

"Can we please just all stay still for a minute?" I say. There are moanings and mutterings, and Mum fusses that her hair's not right, but eventually everyone's in place again.

I hold up the phone. Look at the screen. Then.

Another person comes into shot. She's wearing a red coat. I stop. Lower the phone. The extra person has vanished.

"Oh, come on, Alice, hurry up!" says Theo, who's fidgeting to get back to his football.

"Yes, please, before we all get heatstroke," says Dad.

"Oh, stop being so dramatic, David," says Mum.

"Can you two stop bickering for one second?" I say. Mum pulls a face. Dad folds his arms.

"Great!" I say. "Thanks!"

Looking down at my screen, she's there again—Flo, which of course is short for Florence.

Once I click the button, she disappears for good. Yet what stays is a warm, tingly feeling, because that's what Florence Waterhouse did for me. She made me see hope when everything felt dark. She taught me to believe in fairies.

When I look up, I see Theo, Mum, Dad, and Nell sharing a joke. It's quickly over and they move apart. But at least they're here—we're here—together in the same garden.

Everyone goes back to the table for more cake and tea. All except Theo, who runs about with his football. We talk and eat. But we're all watching him; we can't take our eyes off our little miracle, and perhaps Dad feels it more than anyone.

Not long ago, I thought fairies didn't exist. I didn't believe in ghosts either. And I suppose once upon a time people didn't believe a heart could keep beating in another person's chest. Yet it does. It really does.

About the Author

Emma Carroll is a high school English teacher. She has also worked as a news reporter, an avocado picker, and the person who punches holes into Filofax paper. She recently graduated with distinction from Bath Spa University with an MA in Writing for Young People. *In Darkling Wood* is Emma's third novel. She lives in the Somerset hills of England with her husband and two terriers.